Other books in the

Weary Dragon Inn Series

Ale and Amnesia *(Newsletter Exclusive)*

Drinks and Sinkholes

Fiends and Festivals

Secrets and Snowflakes

Beasts and Baking

Magic and Molemen

Veils and Villains

Zealots and Zeniths

Campaigns and Curses

Perils and Potions

Royals and Ruses

PERILS AND POTIONS

Weary Dragon Inn
BOOK NINE

S. Usher Evans

Sun's Golden Ray
Publishing

Pensacola, FL

Version Date: 9/8/24
© 2024 S. Usher Evans
ISBN: 9781945438943

Map created by Luke Beaber of Stardust Book Services
Line Editing by Danielle Fine, By Definition Editing

Sun's Golden Ray Publishing
Pensacola, FL
www.sgr-pub.com

For ordering information, please visit
www.sgr-pub.com/orders

Dearest cozy reader,

Because this is a cozy book, and so many of you are looking for escape from the usual fare of high stakes, I wanted to warn you that for a brief moment, Bev believes someone to be dead.

Rest assured, he is and will be just fine at the end of the book.

This is cozy fantasy, after all.

~ Sush

Town Hall
Witzel Butchery
Weary Dragon Inn
Library
Town Squa[re]
Mackey Bakery

Pigsend Tea Shop
Flour Mill
Pigsend Village

Chapter One

"Thanks! And, erm, sorry again about…"

"Water under the bridge," Bev said, waving off the latest group of travelers as they departed the Weary Dragon Inn. The trio of young men were on their way to Sheepsburg to find their fortunes and had partaken of a bit too much of the inn's complimentary ale the night before. It had been a while since Bev had had to break out her angry voice, and luckily, the three had taken the hint and gone up to bed. This morning, they were all apologies and offered an extra silver for her troubles, but Bev wasn't one to hold a grudge.

She lingered in the doorway, enjoying the pleasant temperatures for a moment longer. Fall hadn't quite made its arrival yet, but the daunting heat of summer was long gone. In its place were pleasant breezes, warm sunny days, and the occasional rainstorm that watered the still-vibrant foliage—including Bev's beautiful herb garden, which, while it wasn't overgrowing its raised bed anymore, was still thriving as well as it ever had been.

Bev admired it as she washed dirty sheets in a patch of warm sun. Biscuit, her trusty laelaps, dreamed soundly beside her, his tail whacking the ground every so often. To everyone else, he appeared to be a mid-sized dog, with golden fur and eyes, and a few well-placed white spots on his head and feet. But his nose could scent more than bacon; he was capable of sniffing out magic, too, which had come in handy over the past year.

Thankfully, his services hadn't been needed in a while. After a tumultuous election, the small town of Pigsend had returned to quiet, and Bev had returned to the business of running her beloved inn. Travelers were giving her a steady business of at least two or three rooms rented every night, and while there was the occasional grump or too-rowdy patron, most of the time, things were going smoothly.

Bev sniffed the dirty sheets and made a face. It seemed those gents had had a rougher night than she'd anticipated.

Going *almost* smoothly, then.

Bev left the sheets to soak in the suds, wiping her hands on her apron and walking toward her root cellar. Biscuit, who always had an uncanny ability to know when Bev was going near food, woke up and followed, sniffing the dirt floor around the crates of potatoes, carrots, and other root vegetables. Bev had plenty on hand, of course, but she was starting to stockpile what she'd need when all the crops died off in the colder months.

"Perhaps another trip to the farmers' market," Bev muttered to herself. "What do you fancy for dinner tonight, Biscuit?"

The laelaps opened his mouth to unfurl his tongue, smiling happily at her.

"You'll be happy with whatever I give you?" Bev said for him, chuckling to herself. "Good answer, but not quite helpful."

She left the root cellar and returned to the kitchen, finding the recipe cards that her predecessor Wim McKee had left her. Humming to herself, she sorted through them. Beef stew, lamb shank, pork loin, roasted chicken. All scrumptious and delicious, but Bev had made every one in the last week. There was, of course, barley soup, but if she served that tonight, Etheldra Daws wouldn't let her hear the end of it.

She put the cards down and sighed. Every so often, she'd get into these dinner ruts, where the same ol', same ol' wasn't appealing. She tapped the cards then put them away, turning toward the soaking sheets in the backyard, the open door, the soft sound of wind through her herb garden. But she couldn't settle, not when every time the door opened, she held her breath and braced for the worst.

Biscuit nudged her leg, and she reached down to scratch his ears. "Yes, you're right. Shouldn't be acting like I'm waiting for something. Let's get Sin ready and go to the market."

~

Sin was happy for the exercise, though the old mule brayed angrily when Bev momentarily forgot a carrot. When the wagon was hooked up and ready to go, Bev put Biscuit in the wagon next to her and set off down the road.

The day was pleasant, and Bev continued humming to herself. But she couldn't help scanning the countryside, looking for shadowy figures coming out of the woodwork. Catching herself, she cleared her throat and adjusted herself on the seat.

Biscuit whined, and she scratched him again.

"Nothing to worry about," Bev said. "Just a bit unsettled. Things have been too quiet around Pigsend. I'm expecting the next big calamity any minute now."

The wagon rolled over a large, discolored patch on the road, evidence of where the first of many sinkholes had happened almost exactly a year before.

"But all these curiosities happening in town, going all the way back to those soldiers causing the sinkholes… They all happened for a reason. And we're all about to find out what that reason is."

Gore Dewey had said those words to her a few weeks ago, and she hadn't been able to get them out of her head. He'd sent threatening letters to all the candidates running for the mayor of Pigsend—including Freddie, his own candidate—intending to clear the field so Freddie would win, as he had bigger plans for the mayor of Pigsend. Plans crafted by a man named Andres Rade who seemed keen on orchestrating a rebellion against Queen Meandra, and who also might know more about Bev's background than he'd let on during his last visit.

Gore had also said Andres would be back in town soon, hence Bev's nervousness. Vellora, the butcher who lived across the street, hadn't mentioned her commander coming back for another visit, at least when Bev had asked, but there was a real chance Vellora was keeping that information close to the vest to protect him. And a bigger chance Andres, who seemed to be a master of secrets, hadn't told anyone what he was up to.

Biscuit once again nudged her, and Bev came back from her nervous thoughts. "Thanks, Biscuit."

She had to remind herself that today, there was nothing to worry about. There were no mysteries afoot, no strange people in town, no threatening letters or buildings collapsing or sinkholes. There was a pretty blue sky with puffy white clouds, a soft breeze, waving green plants, and the sound of Sin's hooves on the dirt road.

And raised voices.

Bev slowed Sin, turning to look for the source of the ruckus. Two figures stood in a pumpkin patch, yelling at each other with pointed fingers. As this was Herman Monday's farmland, she didn't have to guess who he might be fighting with. Although she probably *should've* kept going, she instead hopped off the wagon and jogged over.

Trent Scrawl, a leathery-skinned farmer with wiry gray hair, stood in Herman's field, red-faced, angry, and bellowing insults. Herman, shorter, squatter, with no hair at all, was doing the same, and it was hard to even hear what they were saying, though Bev distinctly heard, "idiot," "cheat," and "dolt."

"Hey!" Bev called. "You two need to cut this out. What in the world is going on?"

Neither one seemed to hear her, so Biscuit let out a loud bark, which got their attention.

"Oh, Bev." Herman rubbed his nose angrily. "Glad you're here. Maybe you can take this monster off my property before I clock him."

"Clock me? I'm gonna clock *you*!" Trent snapped, advancing again. "You can't tell me those pumpkins are normal, Bev."

He pointed to a patch of extra-large green pumpkins, starting to get a bit of yellow color. They were of varying sizes, but none were shorter than Bev's hip. Bigger than last year's winner, most likely, and definitely enhanced by the magic that had overflowed its banks during the summer solstice.

"I didn't do *nothing* except fertilize and give them love and attention," Herman snapped back. "You remember when those soldiers came to inspect them, eh? Found nothing!"

Bev nodded. They hadn't found *nothing,* per se, and she could understand why Trent thought Herman had cheated. While the magic was natural, the amount of it wasn't, thanks to a pair of herbologists who'd been a little overzealous when planting magical flower seeds. None of that was Herman's fault, though.

"I think that'll be judged at the Harvest Festival," Bev said, after a moment's thought. "If there's anything amiss, the pumpkins will be disqualified, won't they?"

Herman scowled, as if ready to argue, but Trent nodded. "Yeah, suppose they will. Unless this scoundrel did something underhanded to hide the fact that—"

"I didn't do *nothin'* underhanded, you fathead!"

"You two calm down," Bev said, using the same tone she'd used with the rowdy boys the night before. "Trent, you get on back to your own pumpkins. Whoever comes to judge the festival will be as particular as Petula Banks, so I'm sure no one will get away with anything." She turned to Herman. "And shouldn't *you* be at the farmers' market?"

Herman sniffed. "I had a feeling someone would be skulking about my patch today."

"The only one skulking is—"

"Enough, both of you." Bev pointed. "There's nothing else you need to say here. Trent, if I see you on Herman's farm again, I'll get Rustin to have a talk with you."

That was about as lethal a threat as being tickled with a feather, but it worked. Grumbling to himself, Trent stormed off the property.

Herman waited until Trent was halfway down the road to turn to Bev, all traces of anger gone from his face. "Glad you stopped by, Bev. That cur needs a good talking-to once in a while."

"As do you," Bev said. "I thought you two had buried the hatchet after what happened last year with your pumpkins."

He snorted. "Nothing's ever buried with him. But if he knows what's good for him, he'll stay on his side of town. Otherwise, Rustin will be the least of his worries."

Bev had already wasted enough time with the

farmers, so she left Herman to rant and rave to no one about his nemesis and returned to her original task. The market's bounty was finally starting to thin out, which was saying something, as every stand had been overflowing with produce. Now, there were early fall crops like apples, grapes, and even a few small squashes. Alice Estrich, Herman's neighbor, even had a nice selection of yams for the first time, which gave Bev the idea to make some smashed yams for dinner.

"Glad I could be of service," she said as Bev purchased that and all the potatoes and carrots Alice had, which would be stored in her root cellar for the winter months.

"I spotted your neighbor almost coming to blows with Trent," Bev said. "If those two make it to the Harvest Festival without killing each other, it'll be a miracle."

Alice shook her head. "I'm glad I never enter anything in that. Competition makes people do funny things, you know? Happy to sell my wares and be done." She beamed. "I started making some jewelry with woven cotton a few weeks ago. Trying to expand my footprint a little, you know?"

She held up what Bev assumed was a pair of earrings but looked like a poorly constructed spiderweb. "They're gorgeous," Bev said, after a moment. "I'm sure you'll sell hundreds."

"Hopefully not, as I've only made ten so far."

She smirked. "But I hear this year's going to be a big to-do, especially after the mess last year. Is the inn all booked up?"

Bev nodded. "Oh, yes, weeks in advance, as usual. Our judges are going to have to share a room, in fact."

"I'm sure they won't mind."

They'd better not. It was a way to make a little more money for the inn, but mostly Bev wanted to avoid another of the queen's soldiers showing up pretending to be a judge. If they were sharing a room, they might not be able to hide their subterfuge as well. At least, that was Bev's hope.

"Suppose I've got to get back. I have sheets soaking that I need to get out to dry." She tipped her hat. "Thank you for the produce."

Bev loaded up her purchases and headed back to the inn, Biscuit snoozing in the bed of the wagon next to the potatoes. Herman's field was quiet this time, and Bev hoped it remained that way. She thought about telling Rustin to go have a talk with Trent anyway, but then decided against it. The two old men liked to yell and harass each other, but she doubted they'd actually come to blows…

…although they had once before, during the Harvest Festival. That very same queen's soldier who'd been masquerading as a judge had destroyed Herman's pumpkins as he searched for a powerful magical user. Herman had blamed Trent, and the two had boiled over at the livestock judging.

"Well, as long as no one destroys the other's pumpkins," Bev said mildly.

But thinking about Claude—or Renault, as he was really called—drew Bev back to thinking about Gore's warning that it had all been connected. And Bev's fear that Claude, Karolina Hunter, who'd caused the sinkholes, Dag Flanigan, who'd come in search of a dragon shifter, and Zed Mackey, Allen's father and Andres's mortal enemy, had all come to town to find one person.

A person who'd arrived in town at the end of the brutal war between queenside and kingside with a gash on her forehead and no memory of who she'd been before. A person who'd found not one but two amulet pieces, which had given her terrible visions of a bloody battle. That amulet was a wizard's helper, a powerful object that enhanced and honed a wizard's skill.

Bev had buried those fears deep in her mind, but every time a new soldier came to town questioning her past, she became a bit more convinced that everyone knew who she really was. Except her. Even Andres, who'd first told her he had no clue, might've been withholding what he knew, if Gore was to be believed.

"You can ask him next time he's in town. Which will be soon."

"Bev?"

She jumped, pressing her hand to her chest. She was back in the yard of the Weary Dragon, and Ida Witzel, Vellora's wife, was standing there with a smile on her face.

"Goodness me, Ida, you gave me a fright!" Bev said.

"I'm sorry! I thought you saw me. You must've been off in your own world." Ida was lithe and small, with tawny skin and corkscrew curls that were hanging by her cheekbones. She also had the magical strength of three men, but today, she was holding a small clipboard.

"Sorry about that." Bev hopped off the wagon. "Sometimes I get lost in my thoughts on the road."

"Well, driving a wagon's pretty tedious, so daydreaming is allowed." Ida grinned, and it almost looked *too* pleasant. "How are things over here?"

"Good, good," Bev said, growing a little suspicious. She and Ida spoke at least once a day. "How are you?"

"Fantastic. In fact, you're looking at the brand-new chair of the Pigsend Harvest Festival." Ida beamed.

"Weren't you the chair last year?" Bev asked.

"Yes, but you know, Hendry has to choose one every year, so she asked me to do it again."

"And didn't it cause problems with Vellora? Didn't you two—"

"*Bev*," Ida whined. "The appropriate response

here is 'Congratulations, Ida. So happy you've once again been asked to manage a huge festival.'"

Bev parroted the response dutifully, though Ida didn't seem happy at the tone. "Oh, Ida, I'm worried about you, is all. I remember last year quite well. You were a mess, and there was so much consternation—"

"That's last year, what with stray dogs and magic hunters masquerading as pigs and soldiers." Ida waved Bev off. "And I've got a foolproof way to avoid things going wrong this year."

"Oh?" Bev smiled. "What's that?"

Ida beamed at her. "*You.*"

Chapter Two

"Me?" Bev coughed to avoid a snort. "What do you mean *me*?"

Ida beamed. "I asked Hendry if I could have a co-chair this year, and we both agreed that you're the best person for the job."

Bev shook her head. "While I appreciate the vote of confidence, my answer's going to be no."

"If you're worried about being able to enter the breadmaking competition," Ida said, stepping forward hastily, "I checked the rules. As long as you aren't *directly* involved with the judges in any capacity, you're still allowed to compete. First place is yours this year!"

"If Staunton Bucko doesn't come," Bev said.

"Ida, I don't have time."

"Of course you do!" Ida exclaimed. "You're always getting into *something*. Didn't Petula make you an impromptu election monitor?"

"Well, yes, but—"

"Then you've got all the experience you need," Ida said. "It really isn't much. A few meetings, some paperwork to sort though, working with folks around town to make sure there's a place to host all the events."

"All of which sounds like a job for our wonderful, reelected mayor," Bev said gently.

"Bev, *please*?" Ida took her hand. "You have such a way of keeping everyone straight. Not just with all the nonsense that goes on in town, but with your guests. Even Etheldra listens to you!" She squeezed. "Please? For me? Because I'm your best friend?"

"Shouldn't your wife be your best friend?" Bev sighed. "And why aren't you asking her?"

"She's got to tend to the shop while I do…" She gestured. "And don't worry, I've already gotten some help for the week of the Harvest Festival. Not making that mistake twice." She cleared her throat. "Hans Silver said he wasn't doing anything and would be happy to help cover the shop."

Bev smiled but didn't quite feel it. "And how are the Silvers? Freddie, specifically. Still upset about the mayoral race?"

"Surprisingly, he's doing just fine," Ida said.

"Perhaps his heart really wasn't in it, after all."

Bev made a small noise. There were only a handful of people who knew the truth about what had really happened during the mayoral election—including Bev, Wilda Murtagh, Mayor Hendry, Freddie, and Gore. When Freddie realized Gore hadn't only sent letters, but had requested the presence of dangerous magic-hunter Dag Flanigan to investigate all the candidates, Freddie had dropped out, leaving the race between Wilda and Hendry.

"Well, who knows with these things? He could've been like Pip and decided the work was too much," Bev said.

"I think Gore did something, if you ask me," Ida replied. "The two were thick as thieves during the election, and now they won't even talk with each other. It's about as bad as Trent and Herman."

"Yeah, they're already getting into it," Bev said. "I caught them arguing when I was headed to the market. Managed to break it up, but—"

"See? That's why I need you to help, Bev!" Ida exclaimed. "No one else in town could've gotten Herman and Trent to stop arguing."

Bev pursed her lips. Ida really did seem to need help, and Bev did have good luck with the personalities in town. It also wouldn't be terrible to have a distraction from the worry about what might be coming down the path.

She sighed. "What do you need?"

Ida squealed. "Oh, Bev, you don't know how happy this makes me! It really isn't that much of an ask, you know. We've got one big meeting tomorrow afternoon to go over everything we need to do between now and then. After that, we meet every three days until two weeks before the Harvest Festival, then we meet every two days for one week, then the week before, every day, until—"

Bev was already having regrets. "How about this? When we have a meeting, you can come over and get me. I'm sure I'll be able to put down whatever I'm doing and come."

Ida beamed. "Bev, really, this means a lot to me. So much." She clapped her hands. "Now I've got to go find two more people to be on the committee so we'll have a full quorum. Any ideas?"

"Etheldra would probably have opinions," Bev said.

Ida made a face. "Let's not. But Earl, maybe? He might be able to step in. He's all done repairing the town hall."

Bev nodded. "He is busy, though. Lots of folks have been asking him to help before things get too cold again."

"Oh, we're *months* off from colder weather," Ida said with a wave of her hand. "I'm sure he can spare some time."

Bev didn't want to speak for the carpenter, but

she didn't want to argue with Ida either, so she nodded. "Maybe Lillie could help, too? She's not entering the competition. And things at the bakery have finally slacked off a bit. I'm sure she'd be happy to help."

"That's a wonderful idea," Ida said. "I do like her. Is she still living at Wilda's?"

Bev nodded. "I think she's gone for the day, though. That's what Allen told me this morning."

Lillie had, in fact, finally mustered up enough courage to face Merv, her and Bev's mutual friend, who also happened to be a six-foot moleman. Prior to moving to Pigsend, Lillie had lived beyond Merv's door in a safe haven for magical creatures persecuted by Queen Meandra. Pobyds were bakers by nature, and Lillie had chafed at not being able to access wheat flour and fresh fruits for her confections. So she'd stolen the talisman that protected the town, with the intent of breaking the spell keeping her contained. Although she'd come to her senses before causing any real damage, she'd been kicked out of Lower Pigsend for good.

Bev had taken pity on her and helped her restart her life in Pigsend, and to her credit, Lillie had been nothing but helpful and gracious since, even bringing weekly gifts of gold, fruit, and baked goods to Merv's door. The only thing she *hadn't* done was actually speak with the moleman and apologize in person—until today.

"Okay, when you see her next," Ida said. "Allen might also be a contender, but I don't want to ask them both. Someone's got to watch the shops, after all."

"Yes, someone does," Bev said, thinking of all the times she'd be leaving the inn unattended to help Ida. But she did leave the inn unattended a lot, and Biscuit kept an eye on things.

"Best be off," Ida chirped. "Lots to do today!"

~

Bev unloaded the wagon, got Sin back into the stable, and returned to finish the laundry that had been soaking. The stains hadn't quite come out yet, but a few hours in the sun would finish the job. With the sheets blowing in the wind gently, she walked into the kitchen, eager to get back to her favorite part of the day.

Cooler temperatures didn't just mean more pleasant outdoor tasks, but they also meant her bread was back to taking a reasonable amount of time to proof. Per Lillie's suggestion, Bev had been making it the night before then stashing it in the root cellar to proof overnight. When the weather was sweltering, Bev had to pull, shape, and bake it hours before it would be served. But now, she could take the almost-done bread dough from the cellar and let it leisurely continue growing and fermenting until mid-afternoon.

She checked the top of the dough, inhaling the

scent of the flour, yeast, and rosemary, and poked it a few times. All this talk of the Harvest Festival reminded Bev that she'd *almost* won first prize in the breadmaking contest the year before. In fact, judge Petula Banks had said she'd only awarded first place to Middleburg's Staunton Bucko because she'd worried it would give the appearance of impropriety to award it to the woman who'd saved the Harvest Festival.

Still, the blue ribbon was the first thing Bev had ever won (as far as she remembered), and she'd hung it with great pride above the mantel. Now, though, she was itching to get another to hang next to it. First place, if she had her way. Everyone said her rosemary bread—already absolutely delightful—had been taken to a new level by her overnight antics. And the weather would be even cooler during the Harvest Festival, which meant Bev would have even longer to let it ferment and develop the flavors.

"First place, for sure," Bev muttered before Wim's warnings about entering contests and becoming too proud floated through her mind.

Her old boss had about as many opinions as Etheldra, and had taken great pains to fill Bev's empty mind with what he'd wanted her to know. Bread was made this way. The inn was kept so. And six years after arriving, she'd dutifully done most everything he'd said—with the exception of the Harvest Festival entry the year before.

"Well, we'll see what happens."

Around two in the afternoon, the front door opened, and the first guest of the night came walking through. When Bev came out to greet him, she smiled brightly.

"Doc Howser!" she exclaimed. "Goodness me, it's been a while, hasn't it?"

The local doctor ministered to a rather large geographic area, and as such, spent very little time in Pigsend. In fact, the last time Bev had seen him was when Vicky Hamblin had been trapped inside a collapsed house. He'd come two days later to check her out then was on his way again as quickly.

"Too long, Bev." He approached the counter. "Do you have room for an old doctor for the evening?"

"Of course," Bev said. "You don't usually stay in town, though, do you?"

He shook his head. "My home's in Middleburg. Quite central to where I need to go, usually. But Bernard and I are going to be working on some new tinctures this afternoon, so I thought I'd spend the night and head out in the morning. As well as have a slice of that delectable rosemary bread." He beamed. "Tell me you're still making it."

"I've already put it in the oven," she said, looking at her book. No one else had come through yet, so Bev wrote Howser's name on the first line. "Room one. Here's your key. Dinner's at six, but if you're going to be later than that, I can save you a plate."

"You're a gem, Bev." He smiled, his entire face lighting up. "You know, Wim would be very proud of how you've managed this place since his passing. Been four years now, hasn't it?

Bev nodded. "I still can't thank you enough for all you did during that season."

"Dragon pox is nasty business," he said, shaking his head. "The folks down in Litaville just got done with an awful round of it. I was there for three months tending to everyone. Luckily, it wasn't as bad as what hit Pigsend that winter, but we still lost more than we should've." He nodded to the bag he held. "That's why I'm here, actually. Bernard is my favorite apothecary in the area, and I've gotten some new tips on ointments and tinctures that might ease some of the symptoms. Maybe even speed recovery."

"That's wonderful," Bev said. "I know we've all been hoping for a cure."

"If there's anyone to figure it out, it's Bernard." He tapped his forehead. "I'm sure we'll have lots to talk about."

~

Six o'clock arrived, and with it, the usual suspects of hungry diners. Besides three more travelers who'd come through the Weary Dragon's doors to stay the night, there were Etheldra and Earl, Bardoff Boyd, the schoolteacher, and Max

Sterling, the librarian. Doc Howser and Bernard Rickshaw showed up on time, still animatedly talking about options and combinations. It quickly became the focus of conversation across the entire dining room, and even Bev found herself listening closely, especially when Etheldra offered her opinion.

"Well, I daresay that's a dreadful idea," the tea shop owner, who'd confessed to having a semi-magical ability with plants, said to Bernard's idea of mixing undine extract with king's broadleaf, whatever that was. "The two will counteract each other. Better to give the patient water."

"Oh, right, I forgot about that," Bernard said, tapping his chin. "Good looking out, Ms. Etheldra."

They continued throwing around ideas, naming plants Bev hadn't ever heard of before. Even Max, who was one of the smartest men Bev knew, seemed out of his depth.

Midway through the meal, Earl rose and brought his empty plate to Bev. "So, erm, did you get conscripted today?"

"I did, apparently," Bev said with a chuckle. "You, too?"

"Twisted my arm. Hurt, too. You know how strong she is." Earl sighed, looking at Etheldra, who was still interjecting her opinions into the doctor and apothecary's conversation. "But she told me if I wouldn't do it, she'd ask Etheldra. And I can't inflict that on the Harvest Festival."

Bev snorted. Earl and Etheldra were newly married, and while it might've seemed odd that the gentle carpenter would marry such a strong-willed, opinionated woman, they really were quite in love, and Bev was happy they continued to be content in their lives.

"So it's you and me, Ida, and Hendry?" Bev said. "Maybe Lillie."

"Oh, good. I do like her, you know. She's such a dear. And so knowledgeable about baking, too. I'm sure she'll be an asset to all the competitions."

"Just hope Wilda doesn't get any funny ideas," Bev said. She'd hinted quite heavily that she was hoping to utilize her roommate's magical abilities to help her in the pie-making contest. Bev didn't know how she'd react to her roommate being involved in the festival planning. "But at least the election's over, hm?"

"Yeah." His face darkened. "Really wish Pip hadn't dropped out, though. And Freddie! But I guess you never know what people are going through. Pip says he's fine with it. Even complimented Hendry yesterday on stopping by to check on his business without any ulterior motive."

"That's a first," Bev said. The only time the mayor ever saw anyone else willingly seemed to be when she wanted something. "But maybe the election scared her. Made her realize she's got to actually do the work."

"Maybe so." Earl sighed as Etheldra started to get into it with Bernard. "Well, time to get my bride and go, it seems. Bernard makes the tinctures to ease my aching back, so I need him to be willing to sell to me."

Bev laughed as he quickly crossed the room to lead Etheldra from it.

Howser laughed as he rose and brought Bev his plate. "Some people never change. You know, I went to school with Etheldra and Earl once upon a time. Happy they finally came to their senses. He always had a crush on her but never had the courage to say anything."

Bev smiled, taking his plate as Bernard joined him. "Have you two had a fruitful afternoon?"

"Yes, indeed," Bernard said. "Always nice to have Doc Howser in town, isn't it?"

"I feel like everyone can get sick now," Bev said then quickly added, "Except don't, because no one likes being sick."

Howser and Bernard laughed. "I get it. Feels much nicer when there's a doctor nearby," Howser said. "But really, you've got a great apothecary in Bernard. He's practically a second doctor, too."

"Not quite. I don't believe I'm going to be doing any surgery," Bernard said. "Or bandaging wounds. Don't like the sight of blood." He shivered.

"Well, shall we call it a night or get back to it?"

Howser asked.

"I've got a few more hours in me if you do," Bernard said. "I...er...just wanted to ask Bev a quick question."

"Sure thing." Howser tipped his hat and headed to the door.

"What can I do for you?" Bev asked Bernard.

"It's been a while since you've come to see me," he said.

Bev nodded. She really didn't have much use for the apothecary.

"The last time we spoke, you mentioned you'd seen my brother recently."

"Right." Bev shifted uncomfortably. Bernard's brother Gerry was another citizen of Lower Pigsend and had been Lillie's accomplice in the almost-breaking of the spell. His punishment, however, had been to return to the enclave. Perhaps a blessing for him, as he was half-man, half-chicken from a potion gone wrong.

"Have you...heard from him lately?" Bernard asked, a little hopefully.

"Not lately, no," Bev said.

"When you saw him, he was still...feathered, right?"

Bev nodded.

"Suppose the queen's people found him acceptable, then, if he's still causing trouble," Bernard said with a shake of his head.

Bev nodded, not wanting to tell Bernard about Lower Pigsend.

"In any case, I think I've finally managed to make an undoing potion. Something that could turn him human again, you know? I was hoping you might've seen him or know where he's living now."

"I may be able to get a message to him," Bev said. "If you like."

Bernard shook his head quickly. "Now that I think about it, probably not. Best to let sleeping chickens lie, you know? Especially if they're angry brothers who might seek revenge." He took a step back. "Thanks, Bev. For the meal and for…well…"

"Have a good night, Bernard."

Bev watched him go, feeling a little sorry for the apothecary. Gerry had made it clear he still resented his brother, but that resentment might disappear should the other man get the antidote to his own feathering. Bev hadn't really spoken to Gerry since the night Lillie had been kicked out, and she wasn't eager to restart the conversation, either.

Still, the next time she visited Merv, she might as well pass along the message to Gerry, in case he was interested in losing the feathers.

Chapter Three

It was quite late when Doc Howser came back. Bev supposed he and Bernard had continued their cerebral conversations from the night before. Although out of her depth, Bev was quite fascinated with the process of making tinctures, and how the combination of plants could make someone fall asleep or ease their pains or whatever else they were trying to do. And seeing how Wim and the rest of town had suffered during the dragon pox epidemic, a cure was sorely needed.

Howser hadn't yet made his appearance when, at seven on the nose, Lillie arrived with the expected goodies and a bright smile. She was young, in her mid-twenties, with coiled yellow hair and freckles that had only made a reappearance after she'd left the darkness of Lower Pigsend. Today, she wore a bright pink apron, one that seemed knitted instead of the usual cotton ones. Very impractical, but Bev recognized the craftsmanship immediately.

"How was it?" Bev asked. "How's Merv?"

At the mention of the moleman, Lillie burst into sobs, and Bev became alarmed. But when Lillie wiped her eyes, she wore a smile through her tears. "He's magnificent. He was so kind. Forgave me at once for everything except taking so long to finally come see him." She sniffed. "In fact, he told me I needed to make him some of those, erm, cookies again. Said he hasn't gotten a good night's sleep since."

Bev smiled. Lillie had used her pobyd magic to cause the moleman to fall asleep so she could try to break the talisman's charms on his living room. "He's such a generous soul," Bev said. "What goodies did you bring him?"

"Oh, a huge assortment of cookies, some tartlets, a pie." She counted off on her fingers. "Muffins, of course. I was able to go hog wild with the magic, too." She sighed, as if she'd needed to use magic as much as Merv had wanted to eat it. "I don't know which is worse: baking with nut flour or having to hold back my magic." She paused then shook her head. "Nut flour, for sure."

Bev chuckled. "I'm glad you finally went. I hope

you can make it a regular occurrence. And bring me with you next time. Goodness knows I'd like to have a magically laced cookie or two." The ones she'd tasted from Lillie's bakery in Lower Pigsend were still the best things she'd ever eaten. "Just leave out the sleeping stuff."

"Of course," Lillie said. "It was like old times, really. He caught me up on all the gossip in Lower Pigsend. Officer Bola's been demoted. Nog's still keeping a low profile. Shamus is still Shamus, of course, but now that Percival's back to normal, he's a glorified assistant." She cleared her throat. "Speaking of Percival… He showed up, too."

Merv had a charm on his living room to let Percival know when someone walked in; it was helpful to Bev when she came to ask questions. Perhaps not so much for Lillie, who might be keen to avoid the wizard after what she'd almost done.

"What did he say?" Bev asked.

"Well, he thanked me for all the money and supplies I've been bringing," Lillie said, her face turning redder. "I apologized profusely for my role in almost…well, you know." She wiped her eyes. "I told him I didn't want to be let back in, that I didn't deserve it, but if I could send a few letters to some friends, at least… He told me he would allow that. So once I get back home, I'm going to draft them." She sighed. "More apologies, I suppose. I'm getting quite good at them. But he looked wonderful—bright-eyed and powerful, like he was when we all got trapped down there."

The wizard's helper amulet, the pieces Bev had found buried in her garden, now hung around his neck and helped him wield the magic that kept Lower Pigsend humming. Bev didn't like to think about how powerful it made the wizard, especially as that brought up uncomfortable questions about what might happen if *she* wore it around her neck.

"In any case, I feel..." She sighed. "Better isn't the right word. I feel closure, maybe. Percival did so much for me, and he was responsible for keeping me safe all those years I was in Lower Pigsend. That he doesn't think I'm the scum of the earth...well, I might be able to sleep a little better." She winced. "He did say the letters might not be well-received, as my part in the talisman debacle has been widely publicized. But at least I can write them. What happens after that..."

Bev certainly felt for Lillie. Despite her initial anger toward the pobyd for all the consternation caused—both in Bev and Merv's lives, but also in Lower Pigsend—Bev had really grown to enjoy Lillie's company. She'd been intent on proving herself worthy of a second chance, and Bev thought she'd earned it three times over.

"Do you regret doing it?" Bev asked.

"I regret the hurt I caused," she said. "I regret that I made you leave this wonderful place and run around while I watched you without saying a word."

"Yes, that was quite rude of you," Bev said mildly, but with a smile.

"But…I love my life up here," she said, after a moment. "I love that I get to watch the sun rise and the seasons change. I love that I can walk down the street and have my fill of berries and stone fruit and vegetables. And *real flour*, Bev. You don't know what it was like for a *pobyd* to have to use *nut flour*." She sighed. "At least Allen understands that, now."

"And how is, erm, all that going?" Bev asked. "With Allen's new abilities?"

During the solstice, when the magical river had risen to unheard-of levels, Allen's latent pobyd magic had awakened. But unlike everyone else whose enhanced magic had dissipated, Allen had retained his. Since then, Lillie had been coaching him on how to use it in certain circumstances, and how to bake without it.

"He's taking to it like a fish to water," she said with a proud grin. "I daresay with my recipes and his new skills, he'll be able to carry on without me."

Bev's brow furrowed. "You aren't…going away, are you?"

"Not any time soon, but…" She smiled. "I've written a letter to Mr. Abora telling him I'd be happy to move to Silverkeep."

Bev put her hand over her heart. Kemp Abora had been a guest at the inn during the solstice and was scouring the countryside for folks to move to his seaside town of Silverkeep, since they'd been almost wiped off the map by the queen's anti-magic directives. He'd offered Lillie the chance to run her own bakery, but she'd demurred at the time. She'd mentioned a few times that she was thinking about it, but it seemed the pobyd was closer to making a decision than Bev had realized.

"I'll certainly miss you," Bev said.

"Don't fret. I haven't actually *sent* it yet," she said. "But writing it seems to be half the battle. Allen told me I needed to put it in the post the next time it comes to town, but I'm not quite there yet. And once I *send* the letter, it'll take a week for it to even get down to Silverkeep. Then a few days to get a letter back. I'm sure we'd need a month or two to sort through the details." She swallowed, sounding more like she, herself, needed convincing. "In any case, don't mention it to anyone. If it all goes wrong, you know? Maybe Mr. Abora found another baker to move to town in the meantime."

"I don't know. He was quite smitten with your artistry," Bev said. "And I think you'd do well in a new town, too."

"It's rather frightening to leave Pigsend," Lillie said. "Perhaps...even though I know I'm not allowed back, some part of me felt if push came to shove, I could at least hide in Merv's living room. But...the soldiers have come and gone, and none of them pay me any mind. It's making me a little brave. Maybe I can live up here peacefully if I keep my magic to myself."

Bev wasn't too sure about that, but it seemed Lillie wasn't being hasty with her decision. "Have you told Wilda yet?"

"Oh, goodness, no." Lillie shook her head fiercely. "She's been in a foul enough mood as it is since the election."

"I bet." Bev could only imagine. "I haven't seen much of her. Is she planning on entering the Harvest Festival?"

Lillie's landlord, a candlemaker by trade, had entered the pie making contest the year before, though she'd pulled out when her pie had been destroyed by the same queen's soldier who'd destroyed Herman's pumpkin.

"She hasn't said," Lillie said. "I think she's licking her wounds and keeping a low profile. She's taken to delivering her candles in the early morning hours so as to avoid conversation." She tapped her chin thoughtfully. "That is coming up soon, isn't it? The Harvest Festival."

"Ida hasn't found you yet, hm? She's hoping to recruit you to help."

"That sounds like a lot of fun, actually," Lillie said. "Getting to taste all the baked goods. Meeting more people. Is it judging or helping with the coordination?"

"Last time, two judges traveled in," Bev said. "But be warned, one of them turned out to be a queen's soldier in disguise. So that's always a risk."

Lillie chewed her lip. "Yeah, there is always that. Wouldn't it be great if someone knocked her off her throne once and for all, and we could all go back to living like normal?"

Andres, Gore, and Vellora's faces floated through Bev's mind.

"What?" Lillie furrowed her brow. "Someone's not…doing that, are they?"

"I'm a simple innkeeper," Bev said, though that was hard to say with a straight face. "The only plans I care about have to do with running my inn, cooking dinner, and serving bread." She paused. "And submitting that bread to the contest this year."

Lillie brightened. "You're going to win. It's so good. Always has been. Can't believe you lost last year. To what? A rye loaf?" She scoffed. "Outrageous."

"We'll see what the judges say this year," Bev said with a shrug.

One of the upstairs doors opened, and Doc Howser finally made his appearance. He smiled brightly when he spotted the baked goods Lillie had brought and seemed to move a little quicker down the stairs.

"I thought I smelled something delicious," he said as he approached, his hand extended. "I don't think we've met. Doctor Edwin Howser."

"Lillie Dean," she said, taking his hand and shaking it. "I've been helping Allen next door."

"How is young Allen?" Howser asked, concern on his face. "His mother's death really affected him greatly. Though I hear he's been expanding his delivery area."

Bev nodded. "He and Lillie make quite the team."

"He's done a lot of it himself," Lillie said. "You knew Fernley?"

"Oh, yes," he said. "Fernley was a warm soul. Always had a spare cookie for me when she saw me. Said it was for my energy, since I had to travel so much."

"I'm sure we could part with a few," Lillie replied. "I've got a batch in the oven right now. Etheldra won't mind sharing some of her order."

"If they're for her, never mind. Don't want to get on her bad side," he said with a chuckle as he turned to Bev. "Does she dine here every night? I daresay the fifth degree I got last night was a bit more than I'd bargained for."

"She does," Bev said. "But I can tell her to back off, if you need."

"I didn't realize she knew so much about plants," he said. "Though I suppose she did have a good idea or two."

"On occasion," Bev said, leaving out that

Etheldra's knowledge was perhaps helped by her brush with the solstice magic. "I do think married life has made her a little less intense. She's even made Shasta Brewer a full owner in the tea shop. They've got some kind of payment plan happening, and when Etheldra's satisfied, she's going to deed the property over."

"That's lovely," Howser said. "What will she do after she sells the shop?"

"Travel, she says," Bev replied. "But we'll see. I don't know what the town would do without Earl."

"Indeed." Howser sighed. "Did Bernard talk with you about Gerry?"

At the mention of Lillie's accomplice in Lower Pigsend, she stiffened, but Bev nodded. "He asked if I'd seen him lately."

"Have you?"

Bev shook her head, purposefully avoiding Lillie's gaze. "Not for a few months."

"He told me he made a tincture that might undo the...erm...more feathery aspects of his brother's condition, but I'm not sure it'll work. It's so hard to know how to undo something when you don't know how it was done." He tutted. "I think Bernard's worried he's getting up there in years, and wants to make amends with his brother before it's too late."

"I don't think his brother will agree to that," Lillie said.

Howser turned to her. "You know him?"

"Erm." Lillie made a face. "I *knew* him. He was passing through the town I lived in before here," Lillie spoke quickly. "He's not the most savory of creatures. Terrible apothecary, too. Couldn't make a potion to get out of a paper bag, in my experience."

"*Tinctures* is what they're called now, lest we run afoul of the queen's soldiers," Howser said with a knowing nod.

"Right. Tinctures." Lillie's cheeks went pink again.

"And speaking of, we didn't quite get through our experiments last night, so it seems I'm going to need my room for another night," Howser said, turning back to Bev. "Is that all right?"

"Of course. Happy to have you." Bev gestured to the muffins. "Take one for Bernard, too, if you like."

"Don't mind if I do."

Once he was out the door, muffins in hand, Lillie let out a frustrated sound. "Oh, Gerry. I'd almost forgotten about him."

Bev snapped her fingers. "If you do happen to have a few letters to send to the Lower Pigsend crowd, I'll see if Bernard can write one for Gerry, too. Mention the tincture. Not sure how we can get it to him, but—"

"Are you sure that's wise?" Lillie said. "Gerry's…well, he's never spoken highly of his brother. Isn't Bernard the one who turned Gerry into a chicken in the first place?"

"Gerry turned Gerry into a chicken," Bev said. "Because he was trying to poison his brother. Bernard saw through it, switched the vials, and Gerry got what was coming to him." She sighed. "But that was a long time ago. Clearly, Bernard wants to reach out."

"Or maybe the tincture's a potion that'll turn him into a whole chicken," Lillie said with a fiendish grin.

Bev chuckled but shook her head. "Bernard's the nicer of the two, in my experience. But I suppose you never do know what goes on between siblings."

Chapter Four

The rest of Bev's overnight guests came downstairs, took a muffin gratefully, and were on their way, as was usual for the Weary Dragon. Bev tended to their sheets, which were thankfully free of any additional filth, checked on her bread in the root cellar, and put in her meat order with Vellora. Ida was out doing deliveries and pickups today—penance, Vellora said, for her upcoming absences.

"Who do you have helping out again?" Bev asked. "Freddie?"

"Hans," Vellora said. "Seems smart enough. I told Ida I'd see if her cousin Grant Klose wants to come, but she nipped that in the bud quickly."

"That was low, Vellora," Bev said. While Grant

and Ida got along well enough, Grant's family and Ida's family were at odds since their mutual great-grandparents had left the butchery to Ida's side. "But at least she's got help for you."

"Help for the shop, yes, but I have to listen to her talk about Harvest Festival nonsense all evening long," Vellora said. "One of these years, I'm going to have to strong-arm someone else into being chair." She eyed Bev. "Maybe—"

"Don't even think about it," Bev said. "It's bad enough I've been volun-told to be on the committee this year."

"Line up, soldier!" Vellora said, snapping her fingers to attention, perhaps like she had in the war.

It was meant as a joke, but Bev couldn't get Gore's words out of her mind. She hadn't yet asked Vellora, as any mention of the war tended to bring out a darker side in the butcher. And she decided to keep her mouth shut again, as she had a feeling Vellora would feel the need to lie about what she knew of Bev's past, and Bev didn't want to put either of them through that.

"Sorry," Vellora said, perhaps mistaking Bev's falling face for something else. "Old habits, you know."

Bev put on a bright smile. "It's quite all right. I got to thinking of something else for a moment." She adjusted her shoulders. "So what do you have that's good for dinner tonight?"

Roasted chicken would be on the menu, which suited Bev fine. She prepped the birds, added some aromatics of lemon and thyme, then tossed in potatoes and carrots to sop up the grease from the chickens. Biscuit, of course, was very interested in what she was doing, but she had nothing to give him yet, as she wasn't skinning potatoes tonight.

"Soon," Bev said. "I doubt we'll have a full house, so there'll probably be plenty of leftovers for you."

He sat and let out a low *ruff.*

Bev got the chickens and bread in the oven when the back door opened, and Ida breezed in with a bright smile on her face. "Hey there!"

"Ida, hi." Bev turned and wiped her hands on her apron. "I already picked up my meat order. Didn't Vellora tell you?"

"I'm not here about that," Ida said. "It's time to go to your first meeting!"

"Oh, Ida," Bev said, gesturing to the oven. "I've put dinner in. I can't—"

"You're in luck, then," Ida said with a knowing smirk. "Because we're meeting outside your kitchen door."

~

Bev had a sneaking suspicion Ida had done that intentionally, but without any other convincing argument, she followed Ida through the kitchen door into the front room. There she found Mayor Jo

Hendry, Sheriff Rustin, and Lillie sitting around one of her tables. Hendry, pale with a sheet of black hair and blood-red lips, had a thick notebook in front of her that looked eerily similar to the rules and regulations the last Pigsend festival monitor had carried around.

Rustin, broad-shouldered with curly brown hair, leaned back in his chair as Ida and Bev took their seats. He wasn't the sharpest tool in the shed, which was why Bev more often than not had to fix things going wrong in town. That and, as he worked for the queen, one never knew what he might do if he found a dragon shifter, for example.

"I hereby call this first meeting of the Pigsend Harvest Festival Planning Committee to order," Ida said, banging a spoon she'd snatched from the kitchen on the table. "Ida Witzel, chair. Mayor Jo Hendry, vice chair. Bev…erm, Bev Weary Dragon, secretary."

"Absolutely not," Bev said. "I'm here, but I'm not taking notes."

"I can do it," Lillie said. "If you can supply something to write with?"

Bev gave Lillie the quill and ink she used for her guest book, along with a scrap of paper. "Lillie Dean, secretary."

"Rustin, head of security," Ida said. "And Bev, erm… Well, you can't be head of contests, since you want to enter your bread, and if you're not secretary,

I'm not sure there's another job we can give you."

"Great, then I'll go back into the kitchen—"

"She can be vice chair," Hendry said. "I'll manage the contests."

Bev scowled at the mayor, who seemed happy to hand off the job, but Ida noted the changes in her book.

"Wait, what happened to Earl?" Bev said, looking around.

"I couldn't find him today," Ida admitted. "So he's off the hook, I suppose."

Maybe I should've been less easy to find. "I see."

"It's all right. We've got a nice roster here." Ida went back to her book. "Now, we've got a lot of work to do. Luckily, most of this was figured out during the last festival, so we can probably follow the same procedures and be fine."

"Procedures?" Lillie said. "What kind of procedures?"

"Oh, it's a *whole* thing," Hendry said with a drawl. "Last year, before our Harvest Festival planning commenced, I received this ghastly book with all manner of rules and regulations. Typically, it's quite a small affair. But now, we have all these particulars to address. There are sections in here for judging criteria of *anything* we want to host a competition for. Even down to the types of jams allowed to be entered and the criteria for scoring them."

"Goodness me," Lillie said, pulling the book over and leafing through it. "I thought we'd line up the jars and pies and whatnot, have a few people taste them, and decide which they liked best."

"That's how it used to be, too," Ida said with a sigh. "But now we've got to comply with Her Majesty's rules. Because they're sending another festival monitor."

"Not Petula, though, right?" Bev said. Their judge for the last festival had been promoted to election monitor.

"No, they didn't specify who it was." Ida pulled out a letter that seemed to have been read and reread a few times. "But we do have a room for them, don't we, Bev?"

Bev nodded. "They'll have to share, though."

Ida made a face but didn't argue. "I'm sure that'll be fine. It doesn't specify in the rules that they have to have their own accommodations."

"There's a whole section in here about entrants," Lillie said. "We have to keep track of who's entering and where they're from. Didn't we do that for the election?"

"Slightly different criteria," Hendry said with a smirk. "Individuals from other towns who *don't* have a festival already are allowed to enter. Like the poor folk in Middleburg."

"Don't start," Ida snapped at her. "I don't want any funny business during the festival this year.

Least of all from you and whatshername from there."

"Miranda," Hendry said. "No, I daresay we've seen the last of that perfidious mayor. Sent back where she came from with her tail between her legs." She glanced at Lillie. "No offense to your landlord."

"I have no fairy in that parade," Lillie muttered, still entranced by the book. "This says we need to get written agreements from the people whose property we're using. Whose property are we using?"

"We need a few fields to conduct the livestock judging," Hendry said. "I believe we used David Frank last year, didn't we? The pen is still up, to my knowledge."

"Yes, that's where Zed's horses got turned into caterpillars," Bev said.

Everyone in the room stared at her.

"You don't remember that?" Bev said. "During the solstice."

"Was that before or after the magical floating balls of light?" Ida asked.

"Before."

"Before or after the giant chickens?"

"Before." Bev sighed. "In any case, the pen is still there. So I'm sure we can use it."

"Great." Ida scribbled in the book. "Who wants to go talk with him?"

"I can," Rustin said.

"Fine, fine," Ida said. "Remember, we need to

get *written* agreements from him." She slid a piece of paper over to Rustin. "This should suffice. Tell him to sign it then bring it back here."

"But is anyone actually checking any of this?" Lillie asked. "Making sure every entrant has signed paperwork?"

"I didn't sign anything last year," Bev said. "Or this year, for that matter."

"Your paperwork has been filled out for you," Hendry said with a knowing look. "As it was last year."

"Is *that* legal?" Bev asked.

"We're getting off topic," Ida said, waving them off. "So we've got the livestock judging taken care of. The rest of the judging will happen in the town hall, right? Did Earl get it put back together after that fire?"

"Yes. It looks lovely," Hendry said. "One might even say it was a *blessing* the fire started, as the town hall was desperately in need of a fresh coat of paint."

Bev, Lillie, and Ida glared at Hendry, as it still wasn't clear *who'd* set that fire.

"In any case," Hendry continued, shifting a little uncomfortably, "yes, it's set for all the rest of the judging."

"Great." Ida scratched something off her list. "Now, has anyone been in touch with Ramone lately?"

"They went north for the summer based on the

note they left on their door," Bev said. When everyone's heads swiveled in her direction, she sighed. "Fine, I'll zip over there and see if they're still gone. Why?"

"Well, we want the dragon fountain installed," Hendry said at the same time Ida said, "We want them to hold off on the dragon fountain installation."

The two women shared a look before getting into it.

"It'll take up too much room," Ida said.

Hendry countered, "It's our crowning achievement! The town square's been empty without it."

"We could fit three different vendor tents where it sits."

"And we could attract more tourists in the off season to come see it."

"All right, all right," Bev said, holding up her hands. "I'm not even sure they're back in town. If they are, and they're ready to install the fountain, Ida, I'm sure we can fit as many vendors as we need into the town square, even if we have to spill onto the roads a bit."

"You tell Alice Estrich her booth isn't in the center of town," Ida said. "She's making jewelry, Bev."

"Then Alice can be in the center, and someone else will have to spread out, if necessary," Bev said.

"*Or* we can tell Ramone to put it off a little longer."

"Darling, if we put it off any longer, it'll be winter. They've already got far too many stipulations about the weather. Why do you think it's taken us a whole year to get it back up?" Hendry sighed. "I thought we had our window in the early spring, but then *Vicky* insisted on putting her tent in the center of town, and, well…that was a wasted opportunity."

"Well, let's just see if they're in town first," Bev said. "Then we'll readdress the issue."

"Fine." Ida jotted that down. "Speaking of the vendors, there are a few stragglers who haven't submitted their paperwork…"

They continued like that, even as Bev got up to check on the chicken. She dawdled over the pans, hoping she could avoid most of the conversation, but was summarily called back in after only five minutes.

"Something else we need you to check out," Ida said. "We were going through our entrants, and I realized I haven't gotten Trent's entry paperwork."

"Trent Scrawl?" Bev asked, and Ida nodded. "I saw him yesterday. Arguing with Herman over pumpkins, of course."

"Well, he'll be extra sore if he's not allowed to compete," Ida said. "The deadline is today, so if you could pop over to his house and get it, that would be great."

"Can't Rustin do it?" Bev said, gesturing to the sheriff, who was balancing on the back of his chair and staring at the ceiling.

"To be honest, Bev, you're the only one who can handle Trent," Hendry said. "He's so ornery."

"What about Lillie?" Bev said.

"She hasn't a clue where he lives," Hendry said.

"I have chickens in the oven."

"They need to cook. Plenty of time to get over to Trent's house," Ida said with a knowing smile.

Bev sighed. "I don't—"

"Please, Bev?" Ida asked. "It's the last thing we need before we can officially submit our entrants' paperwork to the registrar, and the post is coming tomorrow. Could you please?" She flashed Bev a wide smile. "For me?"

Bev was already doing *a lot* for Ida but finally relented. "What do I need to bring him?"

~

Bev hadn't actually set foot on Trent's farm since the sinkhole fiasco a year ago. She'd passed by many times on her way to Merv's, keeping an eye on the pumpkins as they grew from tiny vines to small nodules to their current size. They were, unfortunately, about a quarter the size of Herman's. She doubted they'd win this year's contest. Then again, there probably wasn't another pumpkin farmer in the area who'd benefited from the magical river like Herman had.

"Oh, well. You win some, you lose some," Bev muttered as she let herself onto Trent's property.

Last time, she'd been here in the dead of night, looking for proof that he'd tampered with Pigsend Creek. Then, she hadn't had any clue about magical rivers or anything like that. The gnomes had said a river, and she'd made an assumption about the only water source in the village.

That being said, Trent *had been* tampering with the creek, draining it so he could water his pumpkins and win the festival contest. Bev hadn't seen the creek's levels lowered since, so perhaps he'd learned his lesson. Or winning the Harvest Festival pumpkin contest had been enough of a balm to his ego.

"Trent?" Bev called, looking around the empty fields. As cantankerous as he'd been at Herman's farm the day before, Bev would've thought he'd be sleeping in the fields again. But he was nowhere to be found.

She continued up the dirt road to his small, wooden house. The windows were open, with lacy curtains blowing in the breeze—a nice touch Bev wouldn't have expected from the farmer. She called his name again to announce herself before rapping on the door.

No one answered.

She knocked again, calling louder. When there was no answer, she turned the knob and poked her head in.

"Trent?"

There was no one in the small living room. No one on the faded couch, nor at the small kitchen table. But there was a pot on the stove that was boiling over. Bev rushed over and pulled the pot off the hot stove with a nearby tea towel.

Now, she was really worried. "Trent?"

She continued toward the back door, which opened onto the fields. But before she got beyond the threshold, she almost tripped.

There was Trent. Staring up at the sky with empty eyes, mouth open, and not breathing.

Chapter Five

Bev wasn't quite sure what happened next. She knew there was a lot of screaming, that she'd run into town somehow, that Doc Howser and Bernard had heard her. She'd somehow conveyed the situation, though she couldn't recall exactly what she'd said. But the message had come across, and Bernard and Howser rushed back to Trent's house with her.

Bernard, thankfully, stayed with Bev on the front porch, holding her hand and letting her catch her breath. After a few minutes, her rational side came back, and she was able to form thoughts.

"Poor, poor Trent," Bev whispered. "He was looking forward to the Harvest Festival, too. I wonder what happened. Maybe the stress got to him."

"Or someone else did," Bernard glared down the street. "I can think of one person in particular who might be interested in making sure Trent didn't enter his pumpkins into the festival."

"Oh, come now, Herman wouldn't do something like that," Bev said with a firm shake of her head. "Goodness, the two of them are more like brothers."

"I wouldn't put it past my brother to do something like this," Bernard said with a scowl.

Bev was about to argue further, when Howser appeared, looking drawn and sad. "What happened to him?" Bev asked. "How did he die?"

"He's not dead," Howser said.

Frowning, she rose quickly. "What do you mean, not dead? He's not breathing. Not moving. What would you call that?"

"He's in a magical slumber," Howser said. "The likes of which I've never seen before. But he's not dead."

Bev didn't know what to think. "A…magical slumber? That's…" She shook her head. "Who could've done something like this?"

"As I said, probably Herman," Bernard said. "Or maybe Eldred Nest and Trent got into a scuffle, too. Or some other pumpkin farmer eager to get a place at the Harvest Festival."

"But to go so far as to put Trent into a slumber?" Bev blew air between her lips. "Suppose we can figure out who did it later. How do we wake him up, Doc?"

"This is way out of my depth," he said. "The good news is that he's alive and should remain that way for a little while yet. But in case someone put him to sleep so they could finish the job, we should move him to the inn where I can keep a closer eye on him." He beamed at Bev. "If that's all right."

It was more than all right. Bernard stayed with Trent while Howser and Bev returned to the Weary Dragon to get her wagon and Sin. As Bev approached the inn, Ida flung open the door to the butchery, rushing over with concern on her face.

"Bev, where the heck have you been?" she said. "I pulled the chicken from the oven, don't worry about that. And the bread, but I'm not sure it was all the way done. Lillie said it was fine. But we waited and waited for you and..." She finally noticed Howser next to Bev. "What's going on?"

"Trent's been…erm…cursed, would you call it?" Bev said to Howser.

"W-what?" Ida put her hands over her mouth. "What happened?"

Howser gave Ida the quick summation while Bev went into the inn. She briefly checked on dinner, finding it all to her satisfaction (or as satisfied as she could be in her current state), and headed to the back to get Sin and her wagon. The old mule protested loudly, as it was quite past the end of her workday, but Bev cooed at her.

"Trent's hurt, ol' girl," Bev whispered, patting her on the nose. "Do you mind?"

Sin let out a low sigh but allowed herself to be led to the wagon. As Bev was finishing up, Biscuit pressed his nose against her shin. Bev knelt and scratched him behind the ears, and he licked her palm. Somehow, it settled her still-racing mind, and she came all the way back to herself.

"Thanks, Biscuit," Bev said. "I don't know why it unnerved me so. But I'm sure we can set Trent right. If Howser can't, maybe Percival knows of something. I bet a forgetting potion would work, too."

"I'll take it from here, Bev," Howser said, coming around the corner. "I'm sure Bernard and I can get Trent into the wagon without you. I've already fetched Rustin, too. But in the meantime, let's just get the poor man settled."

~

It *was* technically Rustin's job to investigate things like this, and Bev was grateful for the excuse to hand it off to someone else. Every time she thought about his pale, unmoving face, her heart sank into the pit of her stomach and her mind raced again. Thankfully, cutting the chicken and the rosemary bread was a good distraction, and when the clock struck six, Bev brought her meal out to a dining room full of hungry folks.

Of course, the town being small and the grapevine being quick, everyone in the room already knew all the sordid details, and had come up with all manner of theories about who might've done it. The general consensus was that Herman had finally had enough of his nemesis, but Etheldra was the loudest opponent of that idea.

"That makes about as much sense as *me* cursing him," she snapped. "And how do we know he was cursed? Maybe he was poisoned."

"What's the difference?" Bev asked.

"Cursed requires someone to cast magic on a person or thing, *obviously*. Poisoned means he ate something with magic." She rolled her eyes. "Goodness, Bev, you, of all people, should know that."

"Well, the end result is the same," Bardoff said, looking uncomfortable. "And we've got no way to wake him up?"

"Howser's working on something," Bev said. "And Bernard."

"Yes, they've been quite busy, so Shasta tells me," Etheldra said, spearing her potato. Shasta's twin sister Stella worked with Bernard at the apothecary. "And busier now that they've got a magical slumberer to wake."

Just then, the door opened, and Howser walked

in, looking red-faced and tired. His face fell as he saw the full room of diners, and he quickly approached Bev. "We've got Trent, but I don't know if we should bring him through the dining room as full as it is," he said in a low voice. "Maybe we'll wait—"

"We're made of strong stuff, Doc," Etheldra said. "Earl, go help them bring Trent in."

Earl, who was already rising, nodded. "Yeah, let's get him upstairs. Which room, Bev?"

"Three's available," Bev said.

"We can put him in my room," Howser said. "So I can keep a close eye on him."

A few moments later, Earl and Bernard huffed and puffed as they carried Trent in—Earl at his feet, Bernard at his shoulders. His head lolled as if he were fast asleep, but the farmer's eyes were open and unseeing. Bardoff sucked in a breath as he covered his mouth, but Etheldra watched with a steely expression as they carefully carried Trent up the stairs.

When they were gone, Bardoff shook his head sadly. "There's too much funny business happening in town lately. And where's Rustin? Shouldn't he be investigating this? He's our sheriff, after all."

"Do you really want *Rustin* looking into this?" Etheldra said. "Bev, what do you reckon? You're the only one in town who can make sense of these things."

"Howser said Rustin's on it," Bev said. "I'm sure he'll be by to check on the patient any minute now."

Rustin *did* show up about an hour after everyone had left. He looked most upset, and when Bev sat with him at her kitchen table, he took a few slices of rosemary bread to calm himself.

"I went to his house, but I didn't see anything out of the ordinary," Rustin said. "You know, they don't train us for this kind of stuff. Poisonings and curses only happen in the big cities—or they used to. My only job is to keep the peace." He sighed as he took another piece of bread. "But if my bosses hear about this, they're going to fire me for sure."

"Are you still on probation?" Bev said.

"Worse," he said. "You remember when Zed was in town? And the whole place was topsy-turvy?"

Bev nodded.

"Well, Zed dropped a line to my superior— especially about me sharing the list of potential suspects with you. They hauled me in a few weeks ago and told me if they get any other complaints, or word of anything else magical in town that I can't handle, they're gonna fire me!" He shook his head. "It's not my fault. Things keep happening. I don't know how to stop them, else I would."

Gore's words came back to Bev, but she shook them out of her mind.

Rustin continued, oblivious of Bev's concern.

"So the less attention I can bring to myself, the better. Just keep a low profile and pretend everything's fine, you know?"

Bev kept her opinions to herself.

"Do you think it's Herman like everyone else? I haven't gone to see him yet." Rustin made a face. "Don't want to, really. He's mean. They both are. But everyone says Herman did it, so—"

"Not everyone thinks that," Bev said softly. "Do you remember the Harvest Festival last year, when Herman's pumpkins were stomped on? He and Trent cried together over it, remember? That's hardly the behavior of someone who'd hurt their friend."

"People do strange things, sometimes," Rustin said. "But until Doc figures out exactly what happened to him, suppose it's all speculation. Is he upstairs with him?"

"I think so," Bev said, nodding to a full plate in the corner. "I saved him a plate, since he hadn't had dinner yet. Maybe you could run up and get him?"

Rustin did so, and a few minutes later, Howser appeared and sat at Bev's kitchen table, tucking in to his meal as Rustin watched a bit forlornly. Bev wished she had something to offer the sheriff, but Biscuit had devoured the rest of the leftovers.

"It's hard to say exactly what happened," Howser said. "Obviously, we've touched him and suffered no ill effects, so I don't believe his condition is contagious. That, of course, leads me to believe Trent was targeted personally. Someone wanted him asleep for some reason—"

"The Harvest Festival," Rustin said.

"In any case," Howser said. "It looks like I'm staying until this mess is cleared up. Bernard went back home to test some concoctions he's going to try on Trent tomorrow. I'm going to visit Mr. Sterling at the library, and if I don't find anything there, I might have to head back to Middleburg to ask around there."

"Oh, don't go there," Rustin said.

Howser frowned. "What do you mean?"

"Erm…" Rustin's pale cheeks colored. "I mean, don't… Well…"

"Rustin's worried about getting fired due to another magical mishap," Bev said.

"I'll try to keep my research purpose to myself, then," Howser said, patting Rustin on the hand. "And hope that Max has something useful for me in the meantime. But honestly, magical maladies are beyond my knowledge. Always have been, even when there were wizards and mages floating about."

"There might be someone else I can ask, too," Bev said with a smile. "I was planning to head that way tomorrow. Hopefully, between the lot of us, we can figure this out."

~

Bev lay awake in bed, unable to sleep. Trent's

face kept flashing through her mind, and although she was trying to avoid thinking about it, it reminded her *very much* of those visions she had of the Battle of Eriwall. That got her thinking about what Gore had said, and how everything was *connected*. If the blacksmith had been telling the truth, then every mess Bev had gotten involved in the past year, even going back to the sinkholes that had plagued the town, had some larger meaning.

Still, Trent was a simple farmer, and the only one who had any gripe with him was Herman. If he was a player in some larger game, he might've just been a means to an end.

She tossed and turned most of the night and rose with the dawn. As she sat on the edge of the bed, Biscuit nudged her softly. She smiled wearily as she petted him. "I'm fine, Biscuit. Going to see Percival today. He usually sets me straight."

He sat, tilting his head. But Bev found that she couldn't even confide the worries that nibbled at her mind to Biscuit. So she put them aside and focused on her morning chores. There was comfort in predictability, and soon, the tension she'd awoken with was gone.

At seven, Allen brought muffins, along with a special cookie that he said was from Lillie. It was still warm, and when Bev took a bite, flavors exploded in her mouth. She took a minute, closing her eyes and savoring the flavor, before grinning at

Allen.

"She did say she was going hog wild in the kitchen," Bev said, wanting to eat the rest of the cookie in one bite and also wanting to eat it crumb by crumb. "Does she have any more? I'm going to visit Merv this morning."

"About Trent?" Allen asked, and Bev nodded. "Good call. I'm sure those, erm, people will be able to figure out what happened to him. Though, has anyone spoken to Herman?"

"I'm sure Rustin has by now," Bev said. "I'm hopeful maybe this once he can take over an investigation instead of making me run around and do it."

"But you're going to visit Merv?" Allen said with a knowing smile.

"I want to wake Trent up, and Rustin won't know anything about a magical curse or coma or sleep or whatever this is," Bev said, a little hotly. "Once Trent's awake, I'm done. Rustin was saying he got in trouble with his superiors for all the mishaps in town, so maybe he can get himself out by actually solving one."

"Somehow, I don't think that'll be the case," Allen said. "I think the queen's people believe no magic is the best magic."

Allen's father Zed certainly did. "In any case, maybe I can swing by Trent's house and see about that paperwork for Ida. I didn't even think about it yesterday." Bev's cheeks warmed. "I was a bit unnerved by the sight of him, to be honest."

"Who wouldn't be?" Allen shivered. "I'm glad my mother insisted I stay home for that war. I don't know what kind of person I'd be if I'd gone."

Probably as haunted as Vellora.

Chapter Six

Bev had a few overnight guests, but once they were gone—and their sheets washed and hung on the line—she put Biscuit in charge of the inn and walked across the street to the bakery. Lillie was working on a three-tiered cake for Kaiser Tuckey, a wealthy businessman who owned a manor nearby, and nodded to an already-packed basket of cookies sitting on the counter.

"Tell Merv I'll be by next week," she said. "And please do pass on any requests for flavors."

"I will," Bev said. "Did you have those letters to deliver to Lower Pigsend?"

"Yes, they're already tucked away in the basket," Lillie said.

"And the letter for Silverkeep?" Allen pressed, giving her a sideways look. "Is that going in the post today?"

"Not yet." Lillie's face reddened. "I'm not ready. So don't tell Merv about my plans yet, please. We've only reconnected. It might break his heart."

The basket safely on her arm, Bev walked out of town toward Merv's tunnel. The path led her by Trent's land, and her gaze lingered on the pumpkins, still pristine and perfect, and his house in the distance. From here, she wouldn't be able to tell if anything was amiss anyway, but she still kept a wary eye as she walked past.

Far beyond Trent's house was the entrance to Merv's tunnel. After almost a year of visits, Bev had finally gotten smart enough to pluck some of the iridescent mushrooms off the tunnel and put them on a second glowing stick she kept at its entrance to light her way, so she wouldn't have to carry her own stick back and forth. She lifted it over her head to illuminate the roots and large rocks that littered the path.

Before too long, Merv's house appeared, complete with an orange door set into mud walls and green shutters. Bev stuck the glowing stick into the nearby wall and rapped on the door.

A moment later, it opened, and Merv, a six-foot moleman covered head-to-toe in black fur, with long claws he used for knitting and a soft pink nose, beamed at her. He ushered her inside quickly, especially when he saw she came bearing cookies.

"Oh, are those from Lillie? She shouldn't have. I mean, she should, because I will eat them, but goodness, what a treat for me!" He picked at the cookies gleefully as Bev settled on the couch. "I can only assume you're here because there's another magical mystery afoot?"

Bev nodded. "I do hope one day I can just come to visit. But things get busy at the inn, and as soon as I think it might be time to pay you another visit, something *else* happens."

"But what would we talk about then?" Merv chuckled. "Before we get into it, I do want to tell you how lovely it was to see Lillie. The sun and weather are agreeing with her nicely, it seems. And that young Allen is doing a roaring business, I understand."

Bev nodded. "I was skeptical at first, but I really have come to love having her across the street. She's been a wonderful addition to the town. And with Allen's magic, I don't know how he could've managed without her."

Merv beamed. "All's well that ends well in my book." He picked up a ball of yarn and a half-finished blanket. "Now. What sort of calamity has befallen Pigsend today?"

Bev told him briefly about Trent's condition, and he tutted sadly.

"Goodness. Well, I'm sure Percival will be along in a moment. He does so enjoy your chats." He nodded to the door to Lower Pigsend, which Bev hadn't been through in months.

"I hardly believe that," Bev said. "Every time I'm here, I'm asking him for something, it seems."

"But you forget, Bev, it's because of the amulet you gave him that Percival is still strong and able to do what he needs to for Lower Pigsend," Merv said.

The amulet. Bev's thoughts turned back to Gore, and Merv knew her too well to let that slide.

"What is it?" he asked.

"I fear things are coming to Pigsend," Bev said. "And somehow I'm the reason."

"Come now, you're being paranoid," Merv said.

But Bev told him about her conversations with Andres, and more recently, Gore Dewey, the blacksmith, and how it seemed they knew more about her past but didn't want to tell her yet.

"That's awfully rude of them," Merv said. "Why not come out and say it? Why all the secrecy?"

"That seems to be the way Andres operates." Bev rubbed her chin. "There's something else, too, something Gore said that's been weighing on my mind. He said that everything that's happened in town is connected—starting with the sinkholes."

"Everything?" Merv tilted his head. "I mean, not *everything*."

"I can see some of it," Bev said. "Claude or

Renault or whatever his name was came to the Harvest Festival looking for a powerful person. But the Witzels, their blackmailer didn't have anything to do with anything. And PJ's transformation didn't, either—"

"Hm." Merv clicked his claws together.

"What?" Bev said.

"I've wondered what caused that immense amount of snowfall this past winter. Coupled with the insanity at the *summer* solstice—"

"That was caused by a pair of herbologists," Bev said. "They'd planted flowers, remember? Plus the full moon solstice. None of that seems related to the queen or the war or any of it."

"Yes, but..." Merv sighed. "I wonder if the magical river disruption started a catalyst. Perhaps the magic coming and going so quickly triggered a latent power in young PJ. And perhaps caused the excess snow." He shrugged. "I daresay your trips to Lower Pigsend to help me out of my mess weren't connected—unless you want to connect it all to one person."

"Me?" Bev said.

"The queen," he replied with a smile. "And her archaic laws about magic. If that wasn't around, the people of Lower Pigsend would be back in their homes, enjoying their existence. Young PJ, too, would be allowed to transform in peace—though nobody ever really wants a dragon shifter around, you know. Vellora wouldn't have had a registrar, the herbologists wouldn't have had to go to great lengths to hide their flowers, and Gore wouldn't have been so keen on making sure Freddie was the mayor of Pigsend."

That was certainly true. "For the longest time, the queen's edicts seemed so far removed from us," Bev said quietly. "Pigsend was quiet. Everyone got along. But in the past year, it seems Queen's Capital is creeping closer and closer. And things that should stay far away are ending up on my doorstep." She snapped her fingers. "The queen had *nothing* to do with Vicky's wedding being cursed."

"Okay, you've got a point there," Merv said with a hearty laugh.

"But everything else…" Bev sighed. "The amulet was found in *my* garden. *I'm* the one with visions. Would it be such a stretch to think that I'm the one they're looking for?"

Merv surveyed her. "Do you want to be the one they're looking for?"

"Of course not," Bev said. "But knowing what's coming is better than being blindsided. Until Andres comes back, I'm not sure I'm going to be able to do much more than speculate. And hope I can figure out what happened to Trent, and that it's not related."

"It's also *entirely* possible there's a reasonable explanation that's much closer to home," Merv said.

"Does Trent have an enemy?"

Bev nodded. "He's a farmer, like Trent. They've had a rivalry over the Harvest Festival for ages. Came to blows last year, but..." She chewed her lip. "I don't see how he'd have that kind of magic."

"Then perhaps it's those Middleburg yahoos," Merv said. "Weren't they causing trouble during the last festival?"

That, at least, seemed more plausible, especially as the mayor of Middleburg had intimated she wasn't finished trying to move the Pigsend event to her town. "I suppose I need to figure out what happened to him, you know?"

"I think—"

Further conversation was halted when Percival appeared with a pop. He wore his usual purple robes and a warm smile. "Bev, dear! What can I do for you today?" He took a seat across from Merv. "Oh, goodness, are these cookies from Lillie?"

He snatched one and gobbled it with as much fervor as Merv had.

"Yes, I hear she came by," Bev said then decided to save that conversation for later. "We've got another incident in Pigsend. Trent Scrawl, a farmer who lives near here, was found...well, not dead, but someone put him in a magical coma."

"That's horrible," Percival said, taking another cookie with a tempered smile. "But goodness, these are delectable."

"I was hoping you could tell me what sort of curse or potion could cause a coma like that," Bev said. "Or if you know of a way we could wake him up."

"Unfortunately, those kinds of sleeps can be caused by all manner of things," Percival said. "And their cures are as varied. Did your friend have anything on him when you found him?"

Bev shook her head. "Not that I saw, but I can go back and take a closer look around his home."

"Here." Percival brandished his wand and waved it in the air. A vial with purple liquid appeared. "This is a simple potion to detect bad magic. Pour a drop on anything and everything that looks out of place—including any food that might've had poison in it. Once you've got it, bring it back here, and I'll see what I can deduce about it." He paused. "But take care you don't touch it yourself."

Bev took the vial, relief welling in her chest. "You're such a helpful friend, Percival. Thank you so much. How can I repay you for this?"

He beamed as his gaze drifted down to the basket. "More of those would be excellent. And— oh, what are these?" Percival removed the stack of letters, eyeing them. "Right. Lillie had asked me to ensure these got to their recipients." He tucked them away inside his long sleeve. "There's still a lot of anger toward her in Lower Pigsend, so I can't say how these will be received."

Bev nodded. "Also, if you wouldn't mind, Bernard—Gerry's brother—says he might've come up with a cure for Gerry's affliction. I'm not sure Gerry would even want such a thing, and Bernard isn't sure it would work, but I figured I would send the message."

"Consider it delivered." Percival sighed. "I have to say, Gerry's not… Well, it's a shame we ended up with *him* in our midst."

Bev smiled. "Perhaps if he ends up unfeathered, you could let him leave? He's not in danger of running afoul of Her Majesty's people without the beak, I don't believe."

"Perhaps so."

~

Bev thanked Percival again, promising to return with more of Lillie's goodies when she found whatever had caused Trent's coma, and left, carrying the vial gently in her hands. It was early yet, and she had things to do at the inn, but she wanted to visit Trent's house before too much time passed. The sooner they could figure out what had caused the coma, the sooner Percival could wake him up and Trent could tell them who'd given him the spoiled goods.

Thankfully, Trent's house was on the way. She didn't bother knocking and let herself in. Once again, she was met with an empty front room. First, she searched for Trent's Harvest Festival paperwork.

She found it, already filled out and ready to go, and tucked it in her pocket.

"Well, that'll make Ida happy," Bev said to herself. But if Trent didn't wake up in time for the festival, the completed paperwork would be a moot point.

Then, she searched every surface for signs of food or drink. Trent was fastidious, and his dated, but nicely decorated house was impeccably clean. Still, Bev took a slow walk around the living room and the tiny kitchenette off the main room.

There was a small loaf of bread wrapped in a tea towel on the table. Bev uncorked the vial and was careful to allow only a single drop to fall onto the loaf. Nothing happened.

"Bread wouldn't betray like that," Bev muttered, corking the vial again.

She opened cabinets and drawers until she found a couple of scraps of dried meat (nothing), a trio of apples (nothing), and a small scrap of hard cheese (nothing). Deciding the kitchen was a dead end, she instead checked the backyard for a root cellar, finding one off to the side. It seemed well-stocked for the upcoming winter, and Bev tested potato, carrot, and apple, but came up empty.

"You know, he could've just had one slice of something," Bev muttered to herself. "And all evidence of it would be currently in his stomach."

She stood at the entrance to the root cellar and

spied the pumpkin patch. If someone was out to sabotage him at the Harvest Festival, maybe they'd laid the curse on the pumpkins he so carefully tended. Bev approached the patch with trepidation then stopped.

They were wet.

She glanced at the clear sky above. Not a single rain cloud in sight.

"Hm."

Bev dug her toe around in the dirt until she found the evidence of Trent's watering system. It wasn't illegal *per se* but when the creek had been low last year, the additional siphoning of water for his pumpkins hadn't helped things. In fact, it had caused miller Sonny Gray to be unable to mill his wheat, as there wasn't enough creek to push his mill wheel.

Following that train of thought, Bev crossed the patch toward Pigsend Creek—just to check things out. She found it running high and well, as it had all summer long. They'd had plenty of rain over the summer, and Trent's irrigation didn't seem to be hurting anything.

Turning on her heel, she walked back to the patch, uncorking the vials and dabbing potion on every one that looked big enough to enter the festival—and each one showed zero reaction.

"Not the pumpkins."

But the bigger question now was who'd watered

them? And why?

Bev squinted across the landscape. From here, she could barely make out Eldred Nest's property to the north and Dane Sterling's to the south. Could one of them have taken pity on their neighbor and ensured his prized pumpkins were well-fed?

A crash echoed from Trent's house behind her. Bev spun on her heel and sprinted toward the house, vial in hand. She dashed through the back door and listened.

"Hello? Is anyone here?" she called.

Silence answered.

Narrowing her gaze, she picked up the fire poker next to the hearth and held it aloft. "Hello? It's Bev, from the Weary Dragon. I'm here...erm..." Why was she there? "Helping Rustin with his investigation. Is someone there?"

This time, a figure burst out from behind Trent's couch, shoved Bev as it passed, and sprinted out the back door. Bev managed to save the vial before it shattered (though she had a feeling Percival might've added some protections to it, as it kept refilling itself), gathered herself, and followed.

"Wait!" she cried.

The figure, who wore a cloak, was ten paces ahead, but Bev was a bit faster. As soon as she could reach, she grabbed the edge of the cloak and pulled. It slipped off the figure, who spun around, red-faced and furious.

No, not furious.
Scared. And crying.
"H-Herman?" Bev blinked.

Chapter Seven

"Herman Monday, what are you doing at Trent's house?" Bev snapped, putting her hands on her hips. After all she'd done to say he wasn't the one, he certainly wasn't looking innocent, coming back to the scene of the crime.

His voice shook as he spoke. "I-I was j-just coming to l-look after T-Trent's p-pumpkins. Keep 'em fed and watered, you know?" He sniffed loudly and wiped his nose with his forearm. "C-can't imagine w-who c-coulda done this to him. And why."

"People are saying—"

His face turned even redder. "I *know* what people are sayin'! And it's lies, all of it. Look at the size of his pumpkins. Do you think he has a chance at this year's festival? The better target woulda been *me*! Mine are gonna win for sure. Ain't no one else got pumpkins as big."

Bev wasn't sure if he was trying to prove his innocence or boasting. "You were arguing with Trent the other day."

"Yeah, because he was sneaking around my property, the ol' cur." Herman sniffed and waved his arms around. "Again, it woulda made more sense for *me* to get poisoned or spelled or whatever happened to him. Trent was on my property. I'm the clear winner of the Harvest Festival. Why would *I* have any reason to hurt Trent? I was here to water the pumpkins."

"The pumpkins are over there." Bev pointed to the patch a little way away. "Why were you in his house?"

Herman sighed as his eyes watered, and his face reddened as he spoke. "I suppose I kinda wanted to be close to him, y'know? Feels wrong to have this empty house. He's usually here banging around, stinking up the place. Not having him here…" His lip quivered. "D'ya think he's gonna be all right? Will he ever wake up?"

"If I can find the thing that got him in this state, yes," Bev said, declining to tell him about the vial. "If you're feeling so awful about it, why don't you give me a hand? The sooner I find whatever caused him to fall into a coma, the sooner he'll wake up and tell us what happened."

While Bev had already gone through the front room, Herman plowed unceremoniously into Trent's bedroom. There, he assaulted the two bookcases, tossing books, vases, and framed flowers to the floor without a care in the world.

Bev watched him suspiciously. She did believe he'd watered the pumpkins, but she also sensed guilt on him. Did he feel guilty for arguing with Trent the day before?

Or was it because *he'd* poisoned Trent after all? Bev couldn't think of a good reason for him to be in the house, missing Trent aside. Could he have come back to take the very thing Bev was looking for?

Was it possible someone was trying to get them *both* out of the contest this year? A similar strategy had been used to try to frame Mayor Hendry during the election. And Herman had a good point about the pumpkins. Herman was going to be the clear winner this year; no amount of fertilizer would grow Trent's entries to that size.

There could also be another angle Bev hadn't seen quite yet—one related to Andres.

She could speculate wildly, but until she found what had caused Trent's affliction, that was all she could do. And that goal seemed further away than ever. Looking around the destroyed house, Bev realized too late this would've been a better job for

Biscuit. If there was something magical here, he'd be able to find it in no time.

"Where *is* my brain?" Bev muttered.

"What was that, Bev?" Herman asked.

"I think I've searched this place to within an inch of its life," Bev said. "Whatever cursed him isn't here anymore."

"Probably ate it, the moron. Don't see any evidence of a plate or anything like that, you know?" He gestured to the empty table. "Probably something he could stuff in his mouth. Unless the culprit came back and hid the evidence."

Bev looked at him plainly.

He swallowed hard. "Just thinking logically." He nudged an overturned book with his foot. "These were Sherry's, you know. These books. She always wanted to be more than a simple farmer's wife."

"Who's Sherry?" Bev asked.

"She was my girl before she was Trent's girl," Herman said. "Forty years ago. But then she decided she didn't want to be a farmer anymore and skipped town. Married a sugar merchant and moved out west, I think." He cracked a smile. "Trent was more tore up than anyone. He'd fixed up his house to her liking, and she still left him."

That certainly explained the pleasant decor and faded maps on the wall.

"Why did she leave you for Trent, if you don't mind me asking?" Bev asked. "You were both farmers."

He snorted. "Trent went on about how he was gonna sell the farm and whisk her away to here and there. But she got tired of waiting and latched onto the first person she could find."

"Married him, though, right?" Bev asked.

He nodded. "So I hear. But you know how the grapevine goes." He sighed, looking up, and his eyes grew misty. "Besides her, Trent's the only one I've ever…well, you know. Loved." His lip grew wobbly again. "Sure, we argue. The Harvest Festival competition gets between us. But he's a brother to me. Brothers fight, you know? They squabble. Get a little dusty here and there. But that doesn't mean…"

Again, Bev couldn't help but feel Herman was being a little too weepy about his friend's condition. "Steady on, Herman. Trent's not gone. He's asleep." She glanced at the clock. "I've got to get back to the inn. The post will be by any minute now, and Ida needs this completed form from Trent."

"Y-yeah. He's gonna need that. Because he's gonna wake up." Herman seemed to be talking to himself more than Bev. "Gonna wake up and lose the Harvest Festival, but he's gonna wake up." He crossed the room and sank down on the faded couch. "If you don't mind, I'd like a few minutes alone in here. To…well, to be."

"I don't think that's a good idea," Bev said,

gesturing to him to get up. "Everyone in town already suspects you, right or wrong. I can't leave you in here to muck about any more than you already have." She pulled him to stand. "C'mon. Let's get you back home. And if I were you, I'd stay there until this all blows over."

"But what about Trent's pumpkins?" Herman asked.

"I'll see about getting Eldred or Dane to tend to them. They're right next door after all," Bev said. "I don't want to see you over here, again, understand?"

To be sure he complied, Bev escorted Herman all the way back to the Weary Dragon before sending him on his way to his farm. He said nothing, avoiding the glances of those who were out in town. Bev gave everyone a brief smile, hoping his appearance with her didn't signal to them that they'd found the culprit.

When she walked into the inn, Biscuit was waiting at the front door, wagging his tail. Bev knelt and scratched his ears. "Got some things for you to tackle, if you're up for it."

Biscuit promptly stopped and stared at her intently, his soft, floppy ears perking up.

"First, go to Trent's house. I left the back door ajar for you. Sniff around for anything magical. If you find anything that might even hint at magic, come get me."

He let out a low ruff.

"When that's done, we'll go over to Herman's house to search his place."

He wagged his tail.

"Okay, run along." Bev rose and opened the door for him. "I'll make sure Lillie sets aside a few magical cookies for you for your efforts."

At the promise of magic, Biscuit scampered out the door and was gone before Bev could say another word.

With that sorted, she checked on her bread, finding it needed a bit longer before she shaped it. In the meantime, she crossed the street to the butcher shop to deliver Trent's paperwork to Ida.

"Oh, I suppose this is the least of our worries," Ida said, taking the paper and adding it to the thick stack on the counter. "I don't know what the festival monitor's going to say when they find out we've got another problem. Poisoning our contestants hardly seems like something they'd overlook."

Bev thought Trent's condition was more of a worry than the festival monitor's opinion, but she kept that to herself. "I searched his house, but I didn't find anything. If it was something he ate, it's long gone."

"Who even has that kind of skill in Pigsend?" Ida said. "I mean, Bernard makes tinctures that can soothe aches and pains, but I daresay the queen made sure nobody around here can do more than that."

"It could've been a cursed object, too," Bev said. "Like Vicky's bracelet."

"Goodness. Well, we certainly are lucky to have you on the festival planning committee," Ida said with a smile. "You know so much about all the possibilities."

Bev couldn't really agree. She felt she was stumbling around in the dark most of the time.

A flash of dark hair breezed by the front window, and Mayor Hendry walked in, her face stoic and serious. "Good, you're here, Bev. What have you learned? I heard you were walking with Herman from Trent's house. Did you catch him in the act? Do I need to send Rustin to his house?"

Bev put her hands on her hips. "I would've *assumed* you'd already done that. Considering their history."

"I haven't, *because* I considered their history," Hendry said with a pointed look. "Besides, weren't *you* the one telling everyone you thought he was innocent? Has something changed?"

"He was at Trent's house watering his pumpkins," Bev said. "Maybe doing something else, too, but I didn't see him take anything. I told him to go back home and stay there. Going to ask Eldred or Dane to keep an eye on Trent's property for him."

"What's to keep him from leaving and going

back to the property?" Hendry asked.

"I put Biscuit on it," Bev said simply.

Hendry opened her mouth then closed it. "Well, if Herman has anything funny, I'm sure that *dog* will find it."

"I don't think we can allow Herman to participate in the festival," Ida said. "He's not... I mean, if he's our prime suspect..."

"I don't think he's the prime suspect, but I don't think he's entirely innocent, either," Bev said, after a moment. "Do we have to submit the festival paperwork today?"

"Yes." Ida sighed. "Just waiting for the post to come through town."

"Send it," Bev said. "By the time the festival arrives, I'm sure we'll have all this sorted."

"We do have our *best* resource on it," Hendry said with a quirked brow.

Ida bit her lip. "I think we should also consider the motive. Someone wanted Trent out of the competition. Herman would definitely want him out—"

"Or someone wanted us to think Herman was the culprit," Bev said. "He's the clear winner, thanks to all that magic over the summer. I doubt anyone else has a pumpkin even close to that size."

Ida made a small noise, and Hendry nodded approvingly, turning to Ida. "Who else is entering the pumpkin contest?"

"Everyone else is from farther out of town," Ida said, thumbing through the stack. "A few from Middleburg, too."

Hendry snorted. "I still think we should've petitioned to bar them from participating, especially after the stunts they pulled last year."

"The townsfolk aren't responsible for what their mayor did," Ida said. "I'll jot down a list of who's in the contest, Bev. I daresay I haven't seen any of them around since last year's festival, but it wouldn't hurt to pay them a visit." She looked at Hendry. "We could send Rustin?"

Hendry sighed, waving her hand. "I don't think that's a valuable use of his time, but fine."

"What do you think he should be doing?" Bev asked.

"Staying out of the way," Hendry said. "If someone *has* poisoned Trent to get him and Herman out of the competition, they'd surely have the cunning to lie to a sheriff like Rustin. Poor dear has plenty of great qualities, but his investigative skills leave a lot to be desired."

"I can't travel all over the countryside asking questions," Bev said, pointedly. "I have an inn to look after."

"*Fine*." Hendry turned to Ida. "Come up with the list. We'll put it to Herman and ask him who else might be keen on winning this year, or who might have a vendetta against them. That will narrow the list, at least." She sighed. "I suppose *I* can make the rounds."

Bev thought that a very good idea indeed, especially as the mayor had empathetic powers and could force people to do what she wanted. "I wonder, too, if we're perhaps looking at this a little too narrowly."

"What do you mean?" Ida asked.

"Well, it's like you said, Hendry," Bev said. "The folks from Middleburg tried to sabotage the festival last year. Miranda Twinsly even told me during the election that she was hoping Wilda would win so she could bully her into moving it."

"I *knew* it!" Ida gasped.

"Water under the bridge," Bev said, waving her off. "But I wonder if this is yet another attempt by them to cause trouble. As Ida said, a poisoned or cursed entrant would catch the attention of a festival monitor. Petula Banks was ready to move the festival after last year's hijinks—"

"Hijinks caused by a member of the queen's service," Ida said with a knowing look.

"Yes, yes." Bev shook her head. "I think it's good to investigate the pumpkin contest, but we should also keep our eyes peeled for something else."

Ida and Hendry watched her with equally smug expressions.

"What?" Bev asked.

"Yes, *quite* a stroke of genius to add you to the

festival planning committee," Ida said with a smile.

Ida made quick work of the pumpkin list, and while Hendry promised to visit the possible suspects, Bev had a hunch she'd get roped into doing something with it. When she returned to the inn, Biscuit was waiting, and based on his lack of reaction, Bev had to assume he'd found nothing of interest at Trent's house.

"Thank you," Bev said, glancing at the clock. "Let's get this bread shaped and the side dishes ready. Once Ida brings the meat over, we'll head to Herman's house."

As soon as the beef was in the oven, Bev and Biscuit walked the well-worn path to Herman's house. Instead of continuing to the farmers' market like she did twice a week, she and Biscuit turned off the main road and walked a dirt path up to his small, tidy house.

She rapped on the door. "Herman?"

No answer.

"Herman, I swear, if you went back to Trent's house..." Bev muttered.

The front door was open, so Bev let herself inside. She peered around, looking for signs he'd been there, and found a much sparser house than Trent's. A single wooden chair sat next to the hearth, with a side table and a book that contained details about Herman's harvest for the year. The small kitchen area was nothing except a wood stove and a single pot—both of which looked unused.

"Herman?" Bev called before looking down at the laelaps. "Can you find him for me?"

Biscuit, who'd been sniffing the floor as if there were something delicious under the floorboard, lifted his nose, scented the air, then walked toward the backdoor.

Where she found Herman Monday, lying face up and staring at the sky.

Chapter Eight

This time, at least, Bev had the presence of mind to keep herself from losing her cool. Biscuit sniffed around Herman's body, while Bev knelt to inspect closer. She still had the vial Percival had given her, but until Biscuit found something for her to pour it on, it was pretty much useless.

"Do you think he grabbed something at Trent's?" Bev asked Biscuit, rolling Herman over onto his stomach to look underneath his body. "Hoisted with his own petard, so to speak?"

As she searched his pants, her fingers brushed something cool and metal. She held her breath, waiting for the magical curse or poison or whatever to come over her. When it didn't, she pulled the metal from the pocket to reveal a golden necklace with a small pendant. She undid the clasp, finding a lock of hair inside.

"Two guesses to whom this belongs," Bev muttered, closing the clasp to make sure the hair stayed inside. Then she turned it over, revealing an engraving on the other side.

TS ♥ *SD*

"Well, that answers that." Herman *had* gone to Trent's, but he'd had something else in mind to take, and it wasn't evidence of the curse.

To be sure, she offered the pendant to Biscuit. He barely acknowledged it.

"So it wasn't caused by this."

She pocketed the necklace, intending to get it back to its rightful owner, and stared at Herman. Like Trent, he certainly *looked* dead. His chest didn't rise and fall; his eyes were open and unblinking to the sky. But his lips were still full of color and his cheeks ruddy.

Biscuit stopped sniffing and sat, looking expectantly at Bev.

"Nothing?" Bev said. "What a mess, Biscuit. No suspects, no evidence, and two victims. Whatever are we to do?"

He let out a low *ruff.*

"Right. Suppose I'd better get Doc and the wagon," Bev said, shaking her head. "Biscuit, you keep searching. There's obviously something here that Herman touched or ate or..." She blew air between her lips. "Something."

Much like Bev, Howser wasn't quite as excited about the second coma patient, although he and Bev talked in low tones as Howser did his own inspection of the farmer.

"Seems to be the exact same thing that got Trent," he said, rising. "What happened?"

"Herman was at Trent's house," Bev said. "I found him sneaking around there. He had this on him." She showed him the locket. "But I touched it and nothing happened to me, so I don't think this is our cursed object. Probably a treasure Herman was hoping to collect for himself while Trent was incapacitated."

"I don't have my glasses," Howser said. "What's that on the back?"

"I think it's Trent and Sherry's initials," Bev said.

"Ah, Sherry Dawes," he said with a nod.

"Dawes...related to Etheldra?" Bev asked.

"Her younger sister," Howser said.

Bev chewed her lip. "Wonder where she is now."

"To the south, so I heard," Howser said, checking Herman's pulse. "I doubt she's involved."

"I'm grasping at whatever I can at this point," Bev said. "Herman said he was at Trent's watering his pumpkins, but he went to get this thing instead.

I wonder if he accidentally touched whatever cursed Trent, too. Then it took a while to take effect."

"Hm." Howser shifted. "I'm not *entirely* well-versed on curses, but they're quite fast-acting, you know? It's not like you touch it, then it takes a few hours. Usually, it's pretty instantaneous."

"I didn't find anything on Herman, other than this locket," Bev said. "Who knows? Maybe someone sent it to Trent with a curse on it, then, knowing Herman would try to steal it, had a second curse for him?"

Howser turned to her with a quirked brow. "That's certainly a theory."

"As I said, I'm grasping here," Bev said. "It's not often I find two cursed individuals without a lick of magic around them. Usually there's a crumb of evidence."

"How would you find magical evidence?" Howser asked.

Bev's cheeks reddened, and she thumbed at Biscuit, who was snoozing at Herman's unmoving feet. "Biscuit's got a good nose for it."

"I see." He shifted, thankfully keeping the rest of his questions about Biscuit to himself. "So both men. Both farmers."

"Both entering pumpkins into the Harvest Festival contest," Bev said, pulling the list of entrants from her pocket. "I was actually going to ask Herman who else in the contest might want him out. Elmo Nickerson won second last year, so maybe he's keen to win first?"

Howser made a dismissive noise. "I know you've been doing this a bit. Bernard tells me you've become quite good at detangling these mysteries, but..." Howser laughed. "Are you sure that someone would go to these lengths to win a Harvest Festival ribbon? It seems like there's something else going on."

"People do strange things where competition's involved," Bev said. "But I'm not ruling anything out. Perhaps Sherry had a third lover in town who was ready to get his revenge." She tapped her finger to her chin. "I'll ask Etheldra."

"Suppose we'd better get him to the inn," Howser said. "Not good for him to sit out in the sun like this."

"Do you still want him in your room?" Bev asked.

"Perhaps not. If you can spare an extra one, we can place them in beds." He sighed as Bev knelt to grab Herman's feet. "Somehow, I feel these two won't be the last of the victims."

~

Together, Howser and Bev loaded Herman onto the wagon and headed back to town without a word between them. Bev thumbed the necklace in her pocket, still unsure if it was connected. She'd been throwing out possibilities when she'd said the locket might've been cursed twice, but it wasn't completely out of the realm of possibility.

As they pulled up to the inn, Ida came out of the butchery, her hands over her mouth for a moment. "Not again, Bev."

"Afraid so," Howser said heavily as he climbed down. "Bev found Herman on his back porch."

"Ida, could you help us get him upstairs?" Bev said. "Room two. Going to move Trent in there as well."

She hesitated, eying Herman. "Are you sure this curse isn't transferable?"

"Not sure it's a curse," Bev said. "And Howser and I were both able to touch him without any ill effects, so you should be all right."

Ida seemed placated by this logic and, with her supernatural strength, lifted Herman by herself and carried him to the room. She popped into Howser's room to grab Trent, and before long, both men were lying face-up in the two beds. Though Bev knew they were very much alive, they still looked quite dead.

"Probably the longest they've gone without squabbling in their entire lives," Ida said, wiping a tear from her cheek as she stood in the doorway with Bev. "What in the world is going on? Did you even get a chance to ask Herman about the other farmers entering the contest?"

Bev shook her head. "No. He was like this when

I got there."

"Didn't you say you'd been with him at Trent's house?" Ida asked. "Maybe he picked up whatever was cursed there. Or maybe some evil person is walking around cursing random farmers and running away before anyone sees them."

Bev certainly hoped *that* wasn't the case. "What do you know about Sherry Dawes? She was Etheldra's sister, right?"

Etheldra was Ida's grandmother's first cousin, which made Sherry family as well. "Goodness, I haven't heard that name in ages," Ida said with a sigh. "She left town decades before I was born. Doubtful even Etheldra hears from her. From what I gather, she was too good for this place."

Bev showed her the lock of hair. "Herman had this on him when I found him. I have a hunch he stole it from Trent."

Ida stared at her, fear in her eyes. "And you *touched* it?"

"Biscuit sniffed it," Bev said. "Didn't find anything exciting about it. So I figured it was safe."

Ida calmed down. "Suppose it's coincidence. Wish they'd wake up and tell us what's going on."

"Yes, that would certainly make things easier," Bev said with a long sigh. "There's a logical explanation. There always is. I think our hunch about the pumpkin farmers is a good one. Hendry will have a longer journey to make—"

"I'm not making *any* journeys," Hendry boomed from behind them. She walked down the hall and peered into the room with disgust on her face. "Of course. Way to throw off suspicion, Herman. Probably did it to himself. Pressure got to him. Took whatever he gave Trent and decided to join his friend in sleepless oblivion."

"What do you mean you aren't going on a journey?" Bev asked Hendry, ignoring the rest of what she'd said. "We need to talk to the farmers and see who might've cursed them."

"Yes, of course, Bev. Instead of *me* wasting *my time*, I sent Rustin to *invite* each of the individuals to town to discuss the incident," Hendry said with a smile. "He's been gone all day delivering notes. They're expected at the town hall tomorrow afternoon, so Bev, be sure to leave some room at the inn for them, as the day may go quite late."

Bev glared at her. "How many are we talking?"

"I'm sure you'll have a full house, dear," Hendry said. "Why are you scowling? It's a good thing. Business is business, isn't it?" She peered inside the room once more. "Poor scoundrels. Well, hopefully one of the culprits will reveal themselves, and we'll be able to revive the two and keep on toward the festival." She turned to Bev. "Are you going to bake something for our incoming farmers?"

Bev stared at her. "What do you mean?"

"Oh, you know you had those scones once, or

what about the lemon-blueberry bread?" She smiled. "Something to force them to talk."

"I was hoping *you'd* do that," Bev said. "It's your specialty, after all."

Hendry sniffed. "I suppose."

"If we're doing interviews, we should get Trent and Herman's neighbors, too," Ida said. "Just in case."

"Good call," Bev said. "Without any real suspects, we might as well cast the widest net possible."

It was a bit later than Bev would've liked, but she got her rosemary bread in the oven and started working on the side dishes for the evening. As she peeled and chopped, her mind drifted to the poor souls lying upstairs. Herman had been adamant *he* was the more obvious target. Had he been right or was he just another unfortunate victim?

All signs were pointing to someone wanting to disrupt the pumpkin contest. She hoped Bernard and Howser could come up with an antidote before anyone else succumbed.

Speaking of the apothecary, he breezed through the front door of the inn as Bev was tipping potatoes into her large stockpot. He was headed up the stairs but stopped when Bev called out to him.

"Ah, there you are," he said with a tight smile. "How are the patients?"

"The same, I'd wager," Bev said, coming out to join him in the front room. "Doc Howser is still up there with them, I think."

Bernard sighed. "We haven't a clue what's come over them, and I'm not really keen on trying a bunch of options, you know? Never know what could react with whatever's got them sleeping and make it worse."

Percival had said the same. "What do we do, then?"

"There's an old trick a master taught me," Bernard said. "It's...well, it's a little off the beaten path. And if any of Her Majesty's soldiers were around, I'd tell you to keep this to yourself, you know?"

Bev knew all too well. "What is it?"

"If you draw a little blood, there are certain... potions that can help narrow down what's in it. It won't tell you exactly, but it'll get you close." He turned to walk up the stairs. "I hope the two gents will forgive me for poking them."

Bev returned to the kitchen and finished dinner. Bernard left soon after he'd arrived, and Bev didn't think she'd see him for dinner, but she still made a little extra in case. She brought the platter of beef stew over mashed potatoes out, much to the delight of the usual diners.

"Oh, a warm meal like this will certainly ease some of my worry," Bardoff said, first in line. "What with Trent, and now Herman. Who's next, I wonder?"

"You aren't planning on entering the Harvest Festival pumpkin contest, are you?" Etheldra said behind him.

He shook his head.

"Then I think you're fine." She all but pushed him out of the way as soon as he finished serving himself. "Wouldn't be surprised if the two of them cursed each other. Or one cursed the other then stupidly got the curse on himself, too."

Bev had considered that. "It's possible it was something or someone else, too." She glanced at Etheldra. "Have you, erm, heard from your sister lately?"

Etheldra snorted. "Not in the past few decades. Last I knew, she was on her fifth husband somewhere west of here. I doubt she'd ever lower herself to set foot in Pigsend again. She was like that, you know. Too big for her britches."

Or was she somehow back and enacting revenge on her two former lovers? It was plausible.

"Though, I suppose she did me a favor," Etheldra continued. "Can you imagine one of those two dolts as my in-laws? Goodness, I'd never live the shame down."

"They're not that bad," Earl said then quieted as his wife scowled at him.

"Do you know anything about this?" Bev

procured the locket, showing it to Etheldra. "I found it on Herman. I think he stole it from Trent. Do you think Sherry sent it recently?

She snorted, turning up her nose. "Sherry's hair hasn't been that color in thirty years, I'd wager." She turned over the locket. "No, if my *very good* memory serves, Trent had this made for Sherry when they got together. Supposedly, she has a matching one with a lock of his hair in it. But my guess is that she sold the silver as soon as she left Pigsend."

"So more likely, Herman knew about it, and wanted a piece of your sister," Bev said, deflating a bit. She hadn't thought it was related, but she'd still needed to see the thought to its conclusion. "Then we're back to square one. No evidence, no suspects. No motive, either."

"Well, some motive," Bardoff said. "They're both entering the Harvest Festival. Maybe someone really, *really* wants to win."

Bev nodded. "Hendry's invited all the pumpkin contest entrants to come to town tomorrow to be interviewed. Ida's gone to get Herman and Trent's neighbors. And we'll see what they have to say." She sighed. "Hopefully, we'll learn something useful."

Chapter Nine

The next morning, Bev checked on Trent and Herman before she went downstairs. The two men were exactly where she'd left them the night before, save a few adjusted hands where Doc Howser had checked their vitals. Their chests didn't move, but at least the doctor had closed their eyes and mouths. From this distance, she could believe they were sleeping.

Biscuit came up beside her, and she let him pace the room, in case something new popped up, but all he found was a crumb of rosemary bread hidden under the bed. She sighed and beckoned him out then got started on her chores for the day. Nothing she could do for them that she wasn't already doing.

At seven, Lillie brought over the morning pastries—flaky spirals filled with custard and a dollop of raspberry jam on top. They were delicious but ordinary, which was somewhat disappointing after the indescribable goodies from the day before.

"How was Merv?" Lillie said. "Get any answers?"

"Yes and no. I spent all day yesterday looking for whatever put them in that state and came up short," Bev said. "Herman stole a locket from Trent, but per Etheldra, Trent's had it for ages. Biscuit found absolutely nothing at both houses." Bev sighed. "I'm stumped."

"That is a puzzler," Lillie said, furrowing her brow. "Is Herman upstairs?"

Bev nodded. "With Trent. They look exactly the same. Howser says they're in a frozen state, so they don't need to eat or drink anything. They could stay that way for fifty years and wake up looking exactly the same as the day they were cursed."

"Has anyone tried kissing them?" Lillie asked, tapping her finger to her mouth.

Bev made a face. "I'm sorry?"

"Well, you know, in the stories, sometimes, true love's kiss and all..." She cleared her throat. "In any case, it's quite strange, isn't it? Usually there's some trace of magic left."

"Usually," Bev said. "Maybe Ida's right and it's someone walking about town cursing people and leaving no trace."

"But why?" Lillie said.

"That's the question, isn't it?" Bev told her about the farmers coming to town to be interviewed. "I hate to say it, but until someone else drops, that's our only lead."

"You think someone else will?" Lillie asked, a little nervously.

"I hope not," Bev said.

"Suppose there never *is* a dull moment in Pigsend," Lillie said. "We were supposed to have another Harvest Festival meeting today, right?"

"I think all that's been paused until we figure out what happened to Trent and Herman," Bev said. "I hope Hendry's powers of persuasion are enough to elicit a confession."

Because she wasn't sure what she'd do otherwise.

~

Ida retrieved Bev midday, saying that all six of the pumpkin contest farmers had come, as well as Trent and Herman's neighbors. A positive sign, though Bev had been halfway hopeful one of them would've skipped out, as it would've given them someone to narrow in on. But Mayor Hendry had a particular set of magical skills, and if anyone had something to hide, she'd be able to suss it out.

"You'd think she'd have used that skill in the past to help," Ida said. "Like when all those buildings were going down over the winter. Or when Vicky's wedding was going nuts."

"You would think," Bev said. "But why do that when she had me to do her dirty work for her?"

"True."

At the town hall, ten farmers—including the six contest entrants, Dane Sterling and Eldred Nest (Trent's neighbors) and Alice Estrich (Herman's neighbor)—sat on the benches, nervously watching each other from their safe distances away. Only Eldred seemed to be relaxed about the whole endeavor. And Rustin, of course, who sat near the doorway, looking about ready to take a leisurely nap.

"Right, you're here," Hendry announced from the front of the room. She had a list in her hand that she double-checked as she rose. "As you've all been told, Trent Scrawl and Herman Monday have been attacked—"

"What?" Dane jumped to his feet.

Alice also jumped up. "Attacked! By who?"

"That's what we're trying to find out," Bev said, glaring at Hendry. "You didn't have to say attacked."

"What else would you call it?" she replied easily. "Now, we'd like to talk with each of you individually."

"Are we suspects?" Elmo Nickerson, one of the pumpkin farmers who lived near Middleburg, asked.

"Not at the moment, but that all depends on what you tell us," Hendry said with a knowing smile. "Let's do this in alphabetical order, shall we?"

She eyed the list. "Alice, you're first."

Alice rose and nervously crossed the room, holding the edges of her shirt as she approached Hendry. The mayor pointed to her office then beckoned Bev and Ida to follow. Once the four were inside—a tight fit, but they made do—Ida closed the door and leaned against it.

"Goodness, I had no idea something happened to Herman," Alice said, her voice growing sad. "Is he all right?"

"He's in a magical coma," Hendry said, clasping her hands on top of her desk. "As is Trent Scrawl."

"My word." Alice covered her mouth. "Did someone fetch Doc Howser?"

"He's in town, thankfully. But what I'd like to know from you, Alice, is whether you saw anything funny at Herman's the past few days."

Alice swallowed. "Only thing… Well, you were there, Bev. Trent was skulking around Herman's pumpkins a couple of days ago. Bev chased him off. Other than that, things haven't been too out of the ordinary around our parts."

Hendry glanced at Bev, and Bev nodded.

"Did Herman mention anything else about the pumpkin contest?" Hendry asked.

"Other than bragging that he was going to win?" She snorted. "No. He was so focused on his pumpkins that he hardly talked about anything else —well, other than Trent. If you asked me an hour ago, I would've said they were the only two in the contest."

Bev watched Hendry, who was scrutinizing Alice. Finally, the mayor shook her head. "Thanks, Alice. You're free to go."

Alice rose slowly. "Do you think we're all in danger? Is someone out there hurting random people?"

"That's what we're trying to find out," Bev said. "But so far, all signs point to the Harvest Festival as being the motive."

"The pumpkin contest, specifically," Ida added, a little hastily. "Thank you, Alice. We'll be in touch if there's anything else we need to know."

~

The next one called in was August Greenfield, who lived close to Middleburg. He was understandably twitchy when he walked in, settling down and holding onto his hat for dear life. His dark eyes darted around the room, never seeming to rest on anyone.

"August, thank you so much for making the trip," Hendry said with a pleasant smile. "I hope it wasn't too daunting for you."

"What's all this about Herman and Trent getting attacked?" he asked, cutting right to the chase. "And what's it got to do with us?"

"I'm merely asking some questions," Hendry said, sitting back.

He let out a nervous laugh. "Then ask away. I have nothing to hide."

"Have you been in contact with Mr. Monday or Mr. Scrawl in the past few weeks?" Hendry asked. Her tone was light, formal, but her hawklike gaze told Bev she would get an answer out of the farmer one way or another.

"N-no. Not really."

"What does not really mean?" Hendry asked, tilting her head.

"Well, I mean." He cleared his throat. "I have a brother who's a sugar merchant. Comes by here often to sell to the bakers. I've…well, I asked him to take a peep at the pumpkins on this side of town. To let me know what I'm dealing with."

"And I'm sure you were horrified to find out they were quite large, hm?" Hendry asked.

"They're not normal." He crossed and uncrossed his legs. "My brother said there was all kinda strange stuff happening in Pigsend a few weeks ago. Large chickens and whatnot. Not surprised Herman's pumpkins got as big as they did."

"And Trent?" Bev asked.

"Trent? Oh, right. Yeah. They're always after each other. Got into a fistfight last year, if I remember, right?"

Bev nodded. "So that's all? You asked your brother to scope out the competition?"

"Yeah, I mean… It's a long way from my farm

to here. If I'm going to lose, might as well know ahead of time. Then I don't have to go through the effort." He thumbed his hat nervously.

"But you still submitted your name," Hendry said, her tone still neutral. "So you must've thought you had a chance, even with Herman's pumpkins as big as they are."

"Second place, for sure," he said with a quick nod.

"You'd come all this way for second place?" Hendry pressed.

"I mean, I'd rather first, but some years, it is what it is." He shifted. "I don't know anything about curses or what might've happened to them. Nor do I have any idea who might be keen on snatching first place."

Once again, Hendry eyed him for a long time before finally waving her hand. "Very well. You're free to go."

It went on like that, the next two farmers mentioning they'd had some kind of scout blow through town, eyeing the pumpkins. From what Bev gathered, the scouting was limited to Trent and Herman alone. No one thought the farmers out of town had any shot at winning, except the farmers themselves.

"Curious," Ida said, sinking into one of the two chairs after Hendry dismissed the second farmer.

"Everyone thinks theirs is second best to Herman's. So if that were the case, why hit Trent first?"

"Throw us off the scent?" Hendry said with a shrug.

Next up was Dane Sterling. He was related to Vicky and Grant Hamblin, who'd both left for Sheepsburg once they'd discovered the existence of their inheritance. He was nice enough, so Bev thought, and sat with an affable smile.

"Just awful," he said with a shake of his head. "I saw Doc and Bernard take Trent away and wasn't sure what had happened to him. Glad to hear he's not, well, gone for good. But goodness, who would do such a thing?"

"That's what we're trying to learn," Hendry said. "Now, what can you tell us?"

Not much. Dane was friendly with Trent, and as Dane wasn't entering his autumn gourds into the Harvest Festival competition, he and Trent had long conversations about the best fertilizer to use on pumpkins and squash.

"How long have you lived next to him?" Bev asked.

"Oh, a long time. My parents owned the house before I did," Dane said. "Why?"

"Do you remember Sherry Dawes?" Bev asked.

He let out a low whistle. "Better be careful uttering that name, Bev. You're likely to wake the gents up from spite alone. Their fight over her was as bad as any get in these parts."

"Do you remember a locket?" Bev had all but put that aside that as the cursed object, but she still wanted to ask. "And if it was Trent's or Herman's?"

"Trent's locket, yeah." He nodded. "He carried that thing around with him all the time. Afraid Herman was going to steal it if he didn't."

"His fears were well-founded," Bev said, clutching the pendant in her pocket. "Did Trent mention anything about getting anything strange in the post or any new deliveries?"

Dane thought for a moment. "The only thing I can remember being delivered to his house lately was a tincture from Bernard."

"What kind of tincture?" Ida asked.

"Well, you know, we're all getting up there in age," Dane said with a chuckle. "Aches and pains and indigestion abound when you get these gray hairs. I picked up some willow tincture for the two of us and dropped it at his house maybe a month ago?"

That was too long to have been any use.

"Very well," Hendry said with a sigh. "Thank you, Dane. If you can think of anything else, let us know."

He nodded and promised he would, then disappeared out the door.

"Do you think there's something to the tinctures?" Ida asked Bev. "Bernard could've slipped something in there."

"But for what purpose?" Bev asked. "And he's the one working all night long to find a cure."

"Out of guilt, maybe?" Ida shrugged. "I don't know, trying to make sure nothing falls through the cracks."

"If we're going after Bernard, we'd better check the medicine cupboards of everyone in Pigsend," Hendry said. "Because I doubt there's a person among us who doesn't have one of his tinctures."

That was true; even Bev had a vial or two stashed away.

"Suppose we'd better get Eldred in here next," Hendry said. "Not looking forward to this one. Gird yourself for conspiracy theories."

When summoned, Eldred marched into Hendry's office, looking put out to be there and not at all nervous. He sat roughly in one of the two chairs and glared at everyone in the room.

"I ain't had nothing to do with this," he growled. "Trent and I don't have a cross word between us. He stays on his land, I stay on mine, and that's that."

"Well, that's wonderful to hear," Hendry said with a thin smile. "Are you often at the border of your land? Enough that you might've seen if someone was on Trent's land?"

"The only two people I've seen on Trent's property lately was Bev," he thumbed behind him, "and Herman, when Bev ran him off. Other than that, ain't nobody running around." He turned in his chair to glare at Bev. "You still keeping up with that moleman? I see you walking by my house at least once a month with a basket."

Bev cleared her throat. She'd thought no one was watching her. "Erm. Yes. We're friends. I take him some goods every so often."

"Yeah, well…he needs to keep his kind below the surface," Eldred said. "You hear? Bad enough we have varmints of the regular size in my gardens. A six-foot moleman—"

"Merv bothers no one," Bev said with a look. "And he's the only one who lives in the area. Other than the sinkholes, he's had no reason to visit the surface and bother your farm."

"Harrumph." Eldred crossed his arms. "I *told* you there were molemen out there. And none of you believed me."

"Back to the topic at hand," Hendry said. "You have nothing else to share about Trent? No one at his property? No one stopping by to investigate anything? No arguments you overheard?" She tilted her head, as if prying into his mind with hers. "Nothing you want to share with us?"

"*No*," Eldred said emphatically. "Nothing except those molepeople. Bev, you say there's only one, but I've seen more. A little man with green skin, a tall young man, too. Sometimes there's a third guy with them. They appear outta nowhere, talk for a minute, then disappear."

"Eldred, I think that's quite enough," Ida said with a nervous laugh.

Clearly, she thought him talking nonsense, but Bev knew he'd witnessed Percival's assistant Shamus coming to the surface to deal with the merchant who brought goods from farther away. Officer Nog, too, was in charge of visiting the farmers' market and bringing back what he could—when he wasn't drunk off excess magic, that was.

"Can you tell us anything about Trent?" Hendry pressed. "What about the last time you spoke?"

"Can't recall, I—"

Before he could finish, a loud commotion echoed from the room beyond. Bev, Hendry, and Ida shared a look of concern before rushing past Eldred to get to the main room. Those who'd already been interviewed had cleared out, but the remaining few had crowded around a single person.

Earl.

"What's wrong?" Bev said, jogging over.

Her heart sank as Earl's tear-filled gaze swept to her. "It's...Etheldra. I think she was attacked like Trent and Herman."

Chapter Ten

Earl led them to Etheldra's tidy little house. The smell of burnt sugar hit Bev first, and she spotted the bubbled-over pot on the stove. Next her gaze fell to the floor where Etheldra lay on her back, face up, as Bev had found Trent and Herman.

At the sight of his bride, Earl broke into loud, unabashed sobs, and Ida had the presence of mind to lead him away, promising that they were going to get to the bottom of things. Meanwhile, Hendry and Bev knelt beside Etheldra and watched her for a moment without speaking.

"Suppose they're going after the orneriest of people in Pigsend," Hendry whispered, her voice thick with emotion.

Bev caught her gaze for a moment and saw unshed tears. "She's going to be fine. If it's the same thing that's got Trent and Herman, we'll figure it out. Bernard's probably close to a cure now, anyway."

"You're right." Hendry took a breath as she looked around. "What happened?"

Bev had managed to get a little bit out of Earl as they walked over. "He said he stepped out for a minute to help Pip Norris with something. Etheldra was working on her pie filling for the Harvest Festival. When he got back, Etheldra was like this, and the filling had boiled over."

Hendry rose and ran her finger along the edge of the pot, wincing a bit before sticking her finger in her mouth. "Strawberry."

"You realize what this means, right?" Bev said, placing a gentle hand over Etheldra's. It was the longest she'd ever been able to touch the tea shop owner.

"Someone's sabotaging the Harvest Festival," Hendry said. "As I thought. This sort of thing stinks of Middleburg, you know."

"Let's not jump to conclusions," Bev said, though Hendry might not be too far off.

She walked around the kitchen, looking for anything half-eaten or out of place. But the entire kitchen was a mess, as Etheldra had several jars of pie filling in various places on the counter. Each had a number on them, perhaps marking a tweak to the recipe. There were also four pie tins on the counter, seemingly in the process of cooling.

Bev's gaze landed on the first place ribbons hanging above the hearth. Etheldra had won the pie-making contest several years in a row.

"First place in pie-making, first place in pumpkins," Bev said. "Who got second in the pie-making?"

"Goodness, I don't remember." Hendry blinked.

"Gilda Climber," Ida said, walking into the room. "Who moved to Silverkeep."

"Maybe she thought it would be fun to terrorize her old town," Hendry said with a chuckle.

"How's Earl?" Bev asked.

"Howser and Bernard were on their way to check on Etheldra. Bernard took Earl to the apothecary to get him something to calm down." Ida shook her head. "Poor dear. He's quite shaken up by all this. I would be, too, if it were Vellora down on the floor." She shuddered. "What have you found?"

"Not much. Like Trent and Herman, it appears she was in the middle of doing something then collapsed." Bev looked around the kitchen. She'd thought if there was a third victim that she'd find some sort of new evidence. But this kitchen was as frustratingly void of clues as the other two had been.

"Shall we add her to the room at the inn?"

Hendry said to Bev. "Or do you think Earl wants to keep her here?"

"Better to keep them all together," Bev said, after a moment's thought. "C'mon, we can get the wagon from the inn."

And Bev could set Biscuit here to hopefully find something useful.

~

Jane Medlam, the mason and Earl's dear friend, had heard the commotion and was already waiting with the wagon. She, too, had tears in her eyes as Ida loaded Etheldra into the back, and sniffed loudly as she turned to the front.

"We'll get her safe and sound to the inn, Bev, don't you worry," Jane said. "Then I'll be back to check on Earl. Poor thing."

"He's over at Pip and Holly's," Ida said. "Or at least that's what Bernard told me when I left them together."

They rolled on, and Bev watched them go with sadness and a little feeling of loss. Not for Etheldra, but because she genuinely hadn't a *clue* what was going on. Hendry left her soon after, and Bev stood alone in Etheldra's home, walking aimlessly as she turned over papers and books in search of something extraordinary.

Biscuit seemed to have sensed he'd be needed, and Bev found him scratching at the front door to Etheldra's house. Once let inside, he sniffed the floors with interest. Bev could only imagine what Etheldra would say if she knew Biscuit was leaving fur everywhere, but desperate times called for desperate measures.

Bev knelt as he came up to her. "I know there are bits of magic all over this house. But did you find anything that might've caused the coma?"

He sat, unfurling his tongue and smiling at her.

"I take it that's a no." Bev rose and sighed, looking around. "Maybe we should head over to the tea shop. Maybe it was something there. I'm starting to wonder if this delayed reaction theory might have something behind it."

Shasta was working at the tea shop, and the grapevine hadn't worked fast enough, so Bev had the unfortunate job of telling her what had happened to her boss. She gasped in horror, dropping the bag of tea she'd been scooping then kneeling to wipe it up as tears fell down her cheeks.

"Oh, oh, goodness me. I thought… with Trent, and Herman… But oh, goodness. Etheldra? Who would want to… Well," she chuckled through her tears, "I can think of a few people who'd want to hurt her, but not like this."

"Is there anything you can tell me about the last day?" Bev asked. "Anything strange or unusual?"

Shasta shook her head. "No, it's been business as usual. We're in the process of drying all our herbs for the winter. Stocking up, you know?"

"Do you source all your teas from the garden?" Bev asked.

"The black and green teas we get in from the west," Shasta said. "But all the herbal blends come from the garden. Etheldra's really keen on that. Says she doesn't like relying on other people."

That sounds like her... "Did you get a shipment of tea in recently?"

"Maybe two months ago?" Shasta said. "Business is slow in the summer months, usually, so we haven't gone through it. But it's going to pick up now that the weather is nicer, so I'm sure I need to put in a new order."

Bev glanced at the floor, where Biscuit was sniffing around. Once again, mild interest from the laelaps. Nothing worth writing home about.

"Do you think Etheldra's going to be all right?" Shasta asked, chewing her lip. "I know we'd talked about selling me the place, but...goodness, I'm not quite ready for it. I'd hoped to have a few more months learning the business side of things."

"She's going to be fine," Bev said. "Bernard and Doc Howser are on it."

"Bernard's been burning the candles at both ends," Shasta said. "Stella says she's had to take over making all the usual tincture orders, as he's become consumed with finding out what happened to Trent and Herman and..." She swallowed. "Etheldra." She shook her head. "It doesn't make *sense*. There's nothing connecting the three of them, is there?"

There was *one* thing. "Did Etheldra ever mention her sister Sherry?"

Shasta opened and closed her mouth. "Etheldra has a sister? News to me."

"She had a little romantic entanglement with Trent and Herman," Bev said. "Left one for the other then left them both high and dry. This was forty years ago, of course, but…it is a thread of connection between the three of them."

"You're better off asking Earl about that," Shasta said. "Etheldra and I talked tea, and even that was a long time coming." She wiped the counter, shaking her head. "If there's anything Stella or I can do, let me know."

Bev thought for a minute. "Earl got a tincture from Bernard, but if you could whip up a calming blend, I'm sure he'd appreciate that, too."

~

With a tin of tea smelling of lavender, vanilla, and cinnamon, Bev returned to the inn, where she was met by Earl, sitting in one of the chairs across from Howser, who was explaining to him what had happened to Etheldra. When Bev walked in the door, they both looked up, hopeful.

"Tea," Bev said, waving the satchel in the air. "How are you feeling, Earl?"

"I'll be better when my girl wakes up," he said with a heavy sniff. "Doc Howser said she's safer here, but I don't know. I'd prefer it if she was at the house with me."

"Just in case there's a nasty turn to this thing we don't see coming," Howser said. "It's better to have them all together."

Earl understood, but still asked Bev if he could spend the night in the other bed. Bev, of course, heartily agreed and waived the fee. As she was settling Etheldra into her room and making sure Earl had all he needed, she delicately broached the subject of Sherry.

"Yeah, it's like she said last night," Earl replied with a shake of his head. "The girls haven't spoken in ages. At least, to my knowledge. Even when they were kids, Etheldra and Sherry never really got along. Too much personality, you know? I think Etheldra was relieved when her sister left the two farmers, as awful as it was for them."

Bev nodded. "You don't think there's a chance the three of them were targeted by Sherry, do you?"

"I can't see a reason for it, no," Earl said. "More likely to do with the Harvest Festival, you know? Etheldra was keen on winning first place again. Maybe someone wanted to get her out of the competition."

"Any ideas who?" Bev asked.

"I haven't a clue who else is entering the pie contest," Earl said. "Etheldra didn't mention anyone, either. You know how she is. Convinced she's going to win."

"She seemed to be testing recipes, though," Bev said. "Is that normal for her?"

He rubbed his chin. "Suppose not. Maybe she felt like experimenting, you know? She does make a mean strawberry pie. And her crust is usually flaky and perfect. But people tinker. You tinkered with your rosemary bread, and it's always delicious."

That was certainly true. "I'm trying to look at all the angles," Bev said. "Last question: did she get a tincture from Bernard recently?"

"You know, she did," Earl said with a nod. "But we both get them from Bernard. Mine for my back and knees, and Etheldra gets a little something to help her sleep. Doubtful Bernard had any cause to poison her, you know?"

"You're probably right, but when was the last time she'd taken the tincture?" Bev asked.

"Last night, probably," Earl said.

With no more questions to ask, Bev thanked him then headed back downstairs. She'd have one less diner this evening, but still needed to cook for the rest of them. As she worked, a couple of overnighters came in, and by dinnertime, Bev found herself fully booked, though only four rooms were paying, including, thankfully, Doc Howser. She was grateful for the extra coin, even if it did mean she had to turn two travelers away.

"Try Middleburg," Bev said, apologetically. "It's

an hour up the road. You're welcome to stay for dinner, if you like, but..."

They declined, grumbling as they left, no doubt exhausted from a long day of travel. Bev certainly hated turning away people, and very rarely had to do it, but she didn't have a choice. As the travelers walked out the door, Ida came breezing in.

"I cross-checked the list of pumpkin contestants with the pie-makers," she said, a little breathlessly as she followed Bev back into the kitchen. "No one overlapped, unfortunately."

"That would be too easy, wouldn't it?" Bev said as she pulled the large pan of meat from the oven.

"Unless they're trying to sabotage the entire festival," Ida said. "That's still very much a possibility." She eyed Bev. "You'd better watch yourself, too, if they're targeting the first- and second-place winners."

"I'll be sure to avoid anything new or strange," Bev said with a chuckle. "Besides that, I'm sure Biscuit would alert me if anything were amiss. Right?"

The laelaps, who was snoozing in the corner, didn't stir.

"Well, in any case, I'm going to tell everyone who got a ribbon last year to be on their guard," Ida said. "But I'm sure it won't be news to most folks. Haven't seen this much chatter in ages. People are saying we should cancel the festival already before anyone else gets struck down." She snorted. "I told Rosie Kelooke I'd cancel it over my dead body."

"Don't say that too loudly," Bev said with a look.

Ida blanched then approached the kitchen table. "Tell me you've got something. A clue, theories, suspects, anything?"

"I have a couple of thoughts," Bev said, turning to the potatoes and scooping them out of the pan. "The first is related to Sherry Dawes."

"Etheldra's sister? But nobody's seen her in—"

"Precisely," Bev said. "But she's connected to Etheldra, Trent, and Herman in some way. Want to make sure I'm not overlooking something."

"Hard to overlook something that's not been around in forty years," Ida said.

"I know, I know." Bev waved her off. "I'm keeping her on the list, just in case. But she's not at the top."

"Obviously, that honor goes to the Harvest Festival," Ida said. "And someone trying to get us to cancel it or move it to Middleburg."

"Right, that is one of the stronger theories," Bev said. "As there's been talk of that even since last year."

"Yeah." Ida eyed the kitchen door suspiciously. "Has anyone spoken with Wilda? Maybe she can shed some light on this whole situation."

"I doubt Wilda would know anything," Bev

said. "Lillie says she hasn't seen her cousin since the election, and she's keeping a low profile."

"Low enough to hide her perfidy?" Ida said.

Bev gave her a sideways look. "I'll go talk with her, but there's someone else I want to speak to first. I'm not saying he's guilty, but I want to ask him a few questions."

"Who?" Ida crept closer at Bev's lowered tone.

"Bernard," Bev said.

"Bernard?" Ida snorted. "The apothecary? Why in the world would he—?"

"It might not be him," Bev said. "But the other connection between the three victims is that they're all Bernard's customers."

"While we're at it, why not investigate the Brewer twins?" Ida said. "Shasta's in line to get the tea shop from Etheldra. Stella works the apothecary with Bernard. Maybe they're in on it."

"But then why attack Trent and Herman?" Bev asked. "I don't think it's Bernard, but I think he may be connected somehow. Maybe someone out to frame him."

Ida let out a small noise. "Oh, now there's an idea."

"The problem is there's no evidence. Even Biscuit didn't find anything, which is doubly strange. I'd hoped another victim would reveal something new, but all it did was puzzle me more."

"Hm." Ida ran her hand over her curls. "Dane

did say he'd delivered a tincture from Bernard to Trent. Maybe Trent got another one." Ida nodded, as if convincing herself. "Maybe Bernard got a bad shipment of some kind of herb, you know?"

"Very possible," Bev said. "In any case, I'm going to talk with Bernard tomorrow and see what he says."

And if Bernard didn't have an answer, Bev would head down to Lower Pigsend and ask Bernard's brother herself.

Chapter Eleven

Dinner was a quiet affair, and not because there were two fewer people. Max and Bardoff wore gray faces as they ate their meals, barely speaking a word to each other. Bev brought a plate to Earl, but when she came back an hour later to retrieve it, it had barely been touched.

"Come now, Earl, you need your strength," Bev said, squeezing his shoulder. "We're not sure how long she's going to be like this. She'll be upset if you aren't here to greet her when she wakes up."

He sniffed and tore off a small piece of rosemary bread. "She's always upset when she wakes up. Says she needs an hour to drink her tea and come to her mind before she can talk." He popped the morsel into his mouth and chewed, then to Bev's relief, tore off another. "I know she's ornery, but she really does have a heart of gold under there. Thinks very highly of you, Bev."

She'd said as much on their wedding day. "I promise, I'm doing everything in my power to wake her and the others up," Bev said. "Is there *anything* else you can tell me about her morning? No detail is too small."

He shook his head. "It was her scheduled day off. She was in the kitchen, like normal. For breakfast, we stopped by the shop and got a cup of tea and a scone."

"And you hadn't seen Trent or Herman at the tea shop, right?" Bev asked.

"I don't think I've ever seen them in the shop, no," Earl said.

Bev chewed her lip. "You don't think Shasta wanted to hasten the transfer of the tea shop, do you?"

"Shasta?" He shook his head. "No, no. She and Etheldra are on good terms." He narrowed his eyes. "You don't think she had anything to do with this, do you?"

"No. I'm just trying to turn every stone I see," Bev said. "Even if I think they're silly."

He promised to eat more of his dinner, and Bev returned downstairs to give him some time. Doc Howser was the only one in the room, slowly spooning the gravy over the roast.

He looked up when Bev appeared on the landing. "Any change?"

"No," Bev said. "Trying to get Earl to eat."

"Good idea." He carried his plate to the middle table and sat. "What a week it's been already."

"You said it," Bev replied, sinking into her chair.

"Are we any closer to finding a culprit?"

She shook her head. "At this point, I'm asking questions of the Brewer twins and Etheldra's long-lost sister."

Howser shifted, only a little. "Sherry?"

"Yeah," Bev said with a nod. "But no one's seen her in forty years. I've heard she's in the north, south, east, and west. Married to a sugar merchant or living the high life as a socialite. Who knows the truth?" Bev chuckled. "But in any case, she's not here, so that's a dead end." She nodded to Howser, who seemed close enough to Trent and Herman's ages. "Are you from Pigsend originally? Did you know her?"

"Erm, yes. I'm from Pigsend. And yes, I did know her," he said. "It was a whole mess, her and Trent and Herman. But it's long since water under the bridge. Forty years is a long time, you know."

"Not for Trent and Herman," Bev said, thinking of the locket again.

"Hm. Well, I'm sure everyone else has moved on," Howser said. "I doubt Sherry, wherever she is, has given those two gentlemen another thought. These two should do the same."

Trent and Herman didn't seem the type to move on from *anything*. "I've got to get to the dishes. Let me know if you need anything."

~

Bev had trouble sleeping, her mind whirring with theories. Each potential culprit seemed more far-fetched than the last, from the Brewer twins plotting the demise of their respective bosses to the far-off specter of Sherry Dawes to Gerry, who was still stuck below ground in Lower Pigsend, per her last conversation with Percival.

There was, of course, the nagging worry that had been haunting her these past few weeks. Gore's words about everything being related sat in her mind like a weight. But what could putting three old people into a magical coma accomplish?

It was still dark when Bev finally gave up and sat on the edge of her bed, rubbing her face and wishing she'd slept a bit more. Biscuit, too, didn't seem ready to wake, as he rolled onto his other side and kept snoring. As she watched Biscuit, she realized there was *one* person in Pigsend who might be able to answer the heaviest question.

First, she popped in to check on Trent and Herman—still the same—then rapped softly on Earl's door, cracking it to peer inside.

"I'm awake," came a soft voice.

Bev opened the door completely and sighed. Earl's eyes were puffy, and based on his disheveled clothes, it looked like he hadn't gotten a wink the night before. "Did you get any sleep at all?"

He shook his head, rubbing his red eyes. "I think I saw her twitch around two. But I'm not sure."

Bev promised to bring him a pastry when Lillie brought them by later and headed downstairs. It was still very early, and most of Pigsend was still asleep, but the blacksmith was usually in the forge early to avoid the hottest part of the day. While she still planned to ask Bernard some questions, and if that didn't pan out, go to Lower Pigsend, first she wanted to speak with the man who'd cursed everyone a month before—just to make sure he and his cohorts weren't behind this again.

As predicted, Gore was hard at work and didn't hear Bev approach. During the solstice, his magical hearing had made itself known for the first time, able to overcome his occupation of working with iron. Gore had heard all manner of conversations and secrets about those in Pigsend—secrets he'd used to blackmail the candidates. But after Freddie dropped out and Gore retreated to his forge, his hearing went back to the normal range. At least, that was what he'd told her.

She waited a few minutes longer, lingering in the doorway before clearing her throat loudly.

"Gore?"

The blacksmith stopped mid-strike and opened the hatch on his helmet, narrowing his eyes at Bev. He replaced the lid and plunged the white-hot iron into the nearby barrel of water, causing a loud hissing noise.

"What do you want, Bev? Here to ask about Andres? Haven't seen him."

"Did you hear about all the magical comas?"

He turned to Bev with what appeared to be honest surprise. "Magical comas? What kind of magical comas?"

"Three citizens of Pigsend struck down at their houses. Doc Howser and Bernard are working on a cure, but we have no clue what actually happened." She paused. "Surely, you've heard about that by now."

"I told you, as long as I'm working here, I don't have any better hearing than anyone else," he said. "I keep my head down and do my work."

"Then have you heard about it in conversations with your…erm…compatriots?" Bev asked.

He rubbed his chin. "Who was struck down?"

"Trent Scrawl, Herman Monday, and Etheldra."

He gave her a sideways look. "That's an eclectic group. Can't say I know why they'd be targeted."

"Does it have anything to do with what you told me after the election? You said everything was connected," Bev said. "Is this?"

"Goodness, you are jumpy," he said with a wry grin. "Did my words get under your skin, Bev?"

"I want to avoid spinning my wheels if I can help it," Bev said impatiently. "So if you have anything to say about this, tell me now before I waste my time."

He chuckled. "No, Bev. As far as I'm aware, these magical comas have nothing to do with our plans."

Bev exhaled, feeling that was truthful. "Thank you." She turned to leave then stopped, his words echoing in her mind. "What do you mean, 'as far as you're aware'?"

"Exactly that," he said. "Andres doesn't tell me everything. What we got cookin' is pretty complex, and people only know their part in the mix. Makes it safer that way, in case someone gets some funny ideas." He turned back to the piece of steel. "You can probably ask Andres the next time he's in town."

"Which will be…"

"As I said, people only know their parts," he said with a wry smile. "See you around, Bev."

Bev returned to the inn, wishing she'd had some closure from her conversation with Gore. What he'd said about keeping things close to the vest did make sense. Andres was dealing with possible rebellions and coups, and that sort of thing tended to attract attention. But it didn't help Bev now.

Lillie brought by pastries at seven, one of which Bev ran upstairs to Earl. Thankfully, he'd finally succumbed to exhaustion and was lightly snoring on the bed. Bev covered him with a blanket before leaving him to sleep. When she came downstairs again, Doc Howser was in the front room, drinking a cup of tea and enjoying one of the muffins. The poor man looked absolutely exhausted but seemed heartened by the pastries waiting for him.

"Any change?" Bev asked.

He shook his head. "It's vexing me greatly. You know, it's easier to watch someone suffer when you know the cause of it and can find a cure. Harder when you don't know what it is." He sighed. "But the hardest of all is when you know what's afflicting your patient and have nothing to help."

"That does sound difficult," Bev said.

"That's why I'm so keen on curing dragon pox. It's such a vicious disease." He sighed, looking up the stairs. "But I suppose that's taken second place to the current problem."

"Has Bernard discovered anything from the blood?" Bev asked.

"Not yet. This is a tricky potion or curse or whatever it is." He sighed. "Now Etheldra's fallen victim to it. Poor Earl. He's such a nice man. Going to make himself sick over her. I tried to tell him that she's in a magical sleep, nothing to worry about.

She'll wake up feeling fine. But I don't think he listened."

"I thought I'd bring one of these muffins over to Bernard," Bev said, pointing to the basket. "Are you headed that way?"

He was, and happily escorted Bev across town, sneaking another morsel from the basket as they walked. Bev couldn't help but notice faces in windows as they passed, all of them suspiciously watching the doctor and Bev. She wished she could tell them there was nothing more to worry about at the moment, but that felt like spreading false hope.

When they arrived at the apothecary, Stella was behind the counter. She wore a thick apron and gloves and was mixing ingredients carefully. She looked up when the door opened and deflated a bit.

"He's in the back," she said, returning to her work.

Bev hesitated, remembering what Ida had said about Stella and Shasta being beneficiaries of the tea shop and apothecary. Could the twins have poisoned Trent and Herman as a diversion when their real intent was to hasten their takeover of the shops?

Stella met Bev's scrutinizing gaze and tilted her head. "What's wrong?"

Bev shook herself. She was getting paranoid. Stella and Shasta wouldn't hurt people like that. "Nothing. Sorry."

She continued to the back room where Bernard was hunched over a much larger table, many more vials and jars and ingredients spread out around him. His hair stuck up on all ends, looking as if he hadn't slept in days, and he was watching the ingredient mixture under a glass.

"Howser, come in. Bev, what can I do for you?"

"Brought some provisions," Bev said, holding up the basket. "Thought you could use a pick-me-up."

Bernard's face lit up, and he quickly took off his apron and gloves. He sighed as he gobbled up one muffin then took his time with the second.

"Yes, that hits the spot. Can't remember the last time I ate anything." He eased himself down onto his chair. "This is a puzzler, I tell you what."

"You said it," Bev replied. "I'm trying to pinpoint a motive, and there are only a few connections between our three victims." She explained her theories about the festival and Etheldra's sister Sherry, the latter eliciting a chuckle from Bernard.

"Yeah, I remember that. They were a few years older than me, but it was the town gossip for a long time."

"And the other connection..." Bev hesitated. Bernard was an even-keeled sort of fellow, but Bev wasn't sure how he'd react to being on her list. "Well, they've all bought tinctures from you."

Worry flashed over Bernard's face "What do you

mean?"

"Well, Dane Sterling told me he delivered a tincture to Trent for his aches and pains. Herman, too, had a few vials of yours at his house. Earl told me Etheldra gets something from you to help her sleep."

"O-Oh, right." He nodded. "Sorry, my brain's a little foggy. Haven't gotten too much sleep while I try to figure this out."

Bev nodded, though she couldn't help but wonder what he'd thought originally. "I don't think that you set out to hurt anyone."

"Of course not. That goes against my entire nature," he said, turning to the muffin.

"But I wonder if someone might be out to get you?" Bev asked. "Do you have any enemies?"

"Other than my brother? None." He shook his head. "I make my tinctures and run my business, you know? It's bad enough I have to keep from running afoul of Her Majesty's soldiers. The rules and regulations on what apothecaries can and can't do are quite numerous."

Bev could only imagine. "You haven't heard from your brother lately, have you?"

"No, but you said you had," Bernard said with a quizzical look. "Do you think he could be behind this?"

"It's entirely possible." Bev didn't want to ask, but she needed to. "And Shasta? How is that going?"

"The dear girl out there?" He chuckled. "You think she's behind this?"

"I'm just asking questions," Bev said.

"Well, I can't say for sure, but I think she's happy," Bernard said with a frown. "She's certainly been getting more practice the past few days, what with me doing all this work back here. But she gets a lot of practice anyway. She'd be ready to take over if she wanted."

"And does she want that?" Bev asked.

He shrugged. "We barely keep up between the two of us with all the orders that come in. I don't think she's in any hurry to be rid of me."

More dead ends, but at least she got those questions answered. Bev glanced at the small vials of blood on the nearby table. "Bernard," Bev began softly. "If one were to bring that blood to someone with, erm…" She cleared her throat. "Magic of some kind or another, would they be able to test it the way you are?"

"They might be able to get something from it," Bernard said. "Why? Do you know of someone with that kind of magic?"

"Maybe," Bev said. "Do you think I could borrow a bit?"

Bernard crossed the room, found an empty vial, and added a few drops of blood to it. "Here you go. If they can figure it out, I would be grateful. I've about exhausted my knowledge of possibilities."

Chapter Twelve

Bernard's worry made her trip to Merv's all the more important. She hoped Percival would be able to glean something from the blood. Even if he could tell her *what* had happened, it might get them closer to the next step. Armed with Lillie's (unfortunately unmagical) pastries and the small vial of blood, Bev headed back to the tunnel to Lower Pigsend.

"Bev! So happy to see you," Merv said, opening the door after Bev knocked. "And are those delicious delectables from Lillie?"

"They are, but they shouldn't have any magic in them," Bev said.

The moleman's face fell, as much as it could behind the thick black fur. "No magic? What's the point of having a pobyd if you don't get enhanced confections?"

"A pobyd living under the queen's rules," Bev said with a look. "Though there hasn't been a soldier in town in a while, but you never know. They like to pretend they're someone else. Better to be on the safe side."

"I suppose." He opened his mouth and ate another muffin. "They're not awful. I'm sure the more I eat, the more I'll get used to them. Unless, of course…" He gave her a look. "They aren't for anyone else, are they?"

"All yours," Bev said. "Though maybe spare one for Percival. I've got questions to ask him." Bev gave Merv the short and sweet version, showing him the vial she'd gotten from Bernard. "Our local apothecary is stumped. He can't even discern the cause for the magical sleep, whether it's a curse or a potion or something else entirely."

"Mm." Merv glanced at the door to Lower Pigsend. "I'm sure he'll be along in a moment. In the meantime, tell me everything that's been going on in Pigsend lately."

Bev told him about the election, filling in the gaps Lillie didn't know, and about the comings and goings at the inn. In turn, Merv told her all about selling his blankets and other woven goods in town, and how he was making a tidy profit. When Bev brought up the Harvest Festival planning committee, and his entering the fiber arts contest again, he demurred.

"No, no. I had my fill of the festival last year." He snorted. "Though I'd hope if I *were* to submit something to the contest, your laelaps would leave it alone this year."

"I'll remind you *Biscuit* didn't eat it," Bev said with a smile. "Claude's magic-sniffing pig did."

"Ah, right!" Merv chuckled. "You're going to enter the bread contest again, aren't you?"

"I was hoping to," Bev said. "But who knows? If we can't figure out who's behind this, we may have to cancel it."

"Perhaps that's what they're after."

Bev nodded. "It seems so strange that there isn't a hint of evidence. I've never been so frustrated in my entire life."

Merv glanced at the clock. "He should've been along by now. It's not like him to take so long."

"Do you think he's still well?" Bev asked.

"Oh, yes. Barring a cold or mild illness, I'm sure he's fine," Merv said.

"Do you think he'd mind it if I slipped down to Lower Pigsend myself?" Bev asked. "I want to speak with Gerry, too."

"Gerry?" Merv made a noise. "Why would you want to speak with him?"

"I want to make sure he's right where he's supposed to be," Bev said, walking to the door. She held her breath, looking back at Merv as she put her hand on the doorknob. It turned over and the door swung open, revealing a dark tunnel. "Well, suppose that's that, then."

"Good luck," Merv said.

~

Bev walked down the tunnel slowly, waiting for something to stop her. But as she'd suspected—as she could still see and access the doorway in Merv's living room—Lower Pigsend was still accessible to her, and before long, she found herself walking along crowded streets full of magical creatures of every sort imaginable.

It would've been easy to get distracted, but Bev stayed true to her purpose. Since she had to assume Percival was busy, she opted to head to Gerry's first. Might as well knock him off her list once and for all.

She passed by Lillie's old bakery, which had been taken over by a cobbler making magical shoes, but from there, her memory was a bit hazy, and she had to stop and ask a passing pair of creatures for directions.

"That monster? Who would want anything to do with him?" The small, pink-winged creature shivered, and a sprinkle of dust came out behind her. "Can't believe he wasn't kicked out with the pobyd for his role in the talisman stealing."

Her friend, a hulking creature with green skin and pointed ears, shook his head. "He's all right at what he does. I get some face cream from him every couple weeks. Don't know if we have another apothecary who could serve that need."

"Oh, Percival could whip something up if you needed it," the pink creature said. "He's so good at what he does."

"In any case, could you point me in the right direction?" Bev said with a hopeful smile.

They gave Bev directions, and soon enough, she stood in front of the apothecary, trepidation coming over her. Inside, a large, yellow-feathered creature was moving about, leaving a trail behind him. Bev swallowed her nerves and walked in, knowing that beneath that feathered exterior, he was a man.

"What'dya..." He spun around, his eyes narrowing. "Oh, it's you. What are you doing here?"

"Have some questions," Bev said. He was only a man, but she still kept her distance. "Have you been up to Pigsend lately?"

"What, the surface?" He scoffed. "Not since that pobyd tricked me into trying to help her."

Bev felt the vial in her pocket. She didn't think it wise to ask Gerry about it, as he'd often been framed as the less intelligent of the two brothers. But as she was there, she could at least ask him what he knew of the maladies.

"We're having another, erm, incident in Pigsend," Bev said. "A few of our locals have been hit by what appears to be a sleeping potion or curse or something."

"How awful." His voice dripped with sarcasm. "I'm sure my brother is working on a cure."

"Indeed, he is," Bev said. "But he said he's coming to the end of his knowledge. Do you have any experience with this? Maybe something that happened down here in Lower Pigsend?"

"We're quite peaceful," he said. "Nobody's going around cursing anyone else. Everyone is grateful to have a place to stay, you know?" He cracked a rueful smile. "The only person who ever wanted to leave was Lillie. How is she doing, by the way? Still causing mischief?"

"She's doing well in Pigsend," Bev said, opting to keep things simple. "Keeping her nose clean and avoiding the queen's soldiers."

"Hmph." He ruffled his feathers, and a few yellow fluffs landed on the floor next to him. "Have you spoken with Percival?"

"I'm on my way there next," Bev said. She'd gotten the sense that Gerry was a proud man and liked to be told he was smart. Perhaps she could use that to her advantage. "But, erm, I wanted to check with you first. Bernard's out of practice in the magical realm."

"Is he?" Gerry quirked a brow. "That's not what I heard."

"What do you mean?"

"Do you have something of the victim's?" Gerry

asked, instead of answering her question. "If you could get me a scrap of clothing, or better yet, a small amount of blood—"

Bev started, her fingers tightening around the vial in her pocket. She only had a little bit of blood, and wanted to give Percival as much as she could to work with. "Erm. I can try to get that. Sure."

"My *dear* brother was trained in the same place I was, so I'm *sure* he's probably already used the same tactics," Gerry said, inspecting his feathers. "Unless, of course, he's the culprit."

"Why would he want to hurt his own clients?" Bev asked.

"Oh, they were his *clients*?" Gerry chuckled. "Maybe he's going senile. Goodness knows, we're not as young as we used to be. Maybe it was an accident. Mixed a wormwood root with a cherry blossom where he should've used willow bark."

"Just one problem," Bev said. "None of the victims had any kind of vial like that on them when they were found. And my laelaps didn't find anything magical, either. It's like they dropped out of nowhere."

"Hmph." He snorted. "I'm sure I *could* help more, but unfortunately, I'm stuck down here. Can't possibly get through Percival's wards and whatnot, you know?" He sighed. "Suppose if you get desperate, you might be able to convince him to let me pop up to the surface and poke around." He waved his wings around. "Preferably without the feathers."

Bev furrowed her brow. "You didn't get the message about—?"

"About what?" Gerry asked, looking at her intently.

Bev thought that quite odd. She was sure she'd told Percival that Bernard might have a cure for Gerry, and that the old wizard had agreed to pass on the message. But, on second thought, perhaps the wizard hadn't shared it because Gerry was still being punished for his role in the talisman stealing.

"When we get desperate, I'll let you know," Bev said, inching toward the door. "Thank you for the chat, Gerry."

"Bring me that blood, if you can," Gerry called after her. "I'd be happy to do what I can."

~

Bev was somewhat suspicious of Gerry's offer—had he poisoned people to get himself a ticket out of Lower Pigsend?—but how could he have managed to get *out* of Lower Pigsend to do it? And what could he have done to the three victims without a shred of evidence? That still remained the largest question, and was why she needed to speak with Percival.

From Gerry's apothecary, Bev headed to the center of the magical enclave. She passed the protective talisman, a shimmering bucket that floated above a fountain. It never ceased to amaze Bev that such a regular-looking item could contain enough magic to hide Lower Pigsend from Her Majesty's forces.

It seemed Percival had become a bit more protective of the talisman, as Officer Bola, a goblin with purple eyes, brown skin, and yellow spots smattered across his forehead, stood in front of it today. He seemed bored out of his mind until he spotted Bev, and marched over wearing a look of consternation.

"What are *you* doing down here?" he demanded. "And how?"

"I walked through the door," Bev said coolly. "I see you've been reassigned."

He scowled, glancing back at the talisman. "Yeah. Important to protect the town, since it's clear *some* people are willing to risk the necks of everyone in town to see a bit of sun."

"Can hardly blame them, especially with all the lies you told the town," Bev shot back. Though she didn't quite disagree about Lillie's behavior, Bola, Nog, and Shamus weren't blameless either, as they'd lied to the people of Lower Pigsend about the ability to come and go. "I suppose this is your punishment and Nog's is going to the farmers' market?"

"Wouldn't call it punishment," he grumbled, but based on the way his face blotched, he probably should have. "But yeah, this is my job. Now I'll ask you again: what are *you* doing here?"

"Percival didn't come meet me at Merv's," Bev said. "I've got questions for him."

"He's not here to be your personal magical question-answerer," Bola replied. "He's a busy man, you know."

Bev did know, and while she didn't love the idea of bothering Percival with her problems *yet again*, it was Bev's amulet (supposedly) keeping him healthy and sane, so she left Bola and continued to the large building where Percival could usually be found. The Merchants House was as crowded as ever, with a long line of people eager to get their wares magically replicated so they could turn around and sell them in the larger marketplace. Bev was once again mesmerized by the sheer variety of creatures before her as she walked along the long queue to the front where Percival's apprentice Shamus was directing people.

He had a clipboard and a harried look on his face as he spoke to the person at the front of the line. When Bev approached, his scowl deepened.

"What are you doing here?" he asked.

"Percival didn't come to Merv's," Bev said. "Is he all right?"

"Fine, fine. Busy." He turned back to his clipboard. "If you have something to ask him, you can get to the back of the line."

Bev was about to argue when the wizard himself

emerged from the back room. To Bev's relief, he looked completely normal and healthy.

"Ah, Bev. So sorry I was detained. Had a tricky bit of magic to sort through. But good to know you found your way." He beckoned her. "Come, come."

Bev gave Shamus a sideways look then followed the wizard back inside his small room. Floating candles lit the space, rotating slowly around the room. Percival took a seat in a purple chair and beamed at Bev.

"Now, what news from Pigsend? Have you discovered anything more about the victims?"

"No, and that's what's new." Bev told him everything, and he listened intently. "Bernard, our apothecary, took some blood from Trent, hoping maybe it would lead him to the answer. But so far, it hasn't." Bev handed him the vial. "I hoped maybe you could see something he couldn't."

Percival inspected the vial. "You said your apothecary is trying to find the magic in the blood?"

Bev nodded.

"That's interesting."

"Why?"

"Well, that sort of tactic veers a little *too* far into the magical, in my view. The kinds of ingredients you'd have to use, the combinations..." He shook his head. "I thought the queen had cleared out all the magical apothecaries."

"Bernard doesn't have magic, to my

knowledge," Bev said. "But, erm… Gerry hasn't been taking any trips to the surface, has he?"

"No. He's been quietly in his shop," Percival said. "The only one who's been out and about in the upper world is Officer Nog to get fresh produce from the farmers' market."

Bev had seen the goblin coming and going. "He wouldn't be able to cast this kind of magic, right? I mean, he was only able to transform the horses and weapons during the solstice due to the excess magic."

"Right," Percival said. "Well, let's see what kind of magic we're dealing with."

He waved his wand, and swirls of purple magic enveloped the vial. After a moment, a poof of smoke rose, which Bev didn't understand, but Percival seemed to.

"Hm." He tilted his head. "That's interesting."

"What?" Bev asked.

"Well, I can definitively say it's *not* a potion," he said. "It's a potion-enhanced curse."

"What's the difference?" Bev asked.

Percival collected his thoughts for a moment. "As we've discussed previously, curses are powerful things. An object can be cursed, travel long distances, and still be as potent. But directly cursing a person requires the wielder both to be in close proximity and to have enough magic to make the curse stick." He gestured to the puff of magic still in the air. "The magic itself comes from a mage or something similar, but the user doesn't have enough. So they've taken a potion or three that enhances their magic to the point where they can cast."

"That would explain why no one's noticed a wizard walking around," Bev said. "So someone could down a potion, enhance their magic, cast a curse, then their magic would disappear?"

He nodded. "The better question is why would someone do that?"

Bev didn't know, but it didn't make her job any easier. "Is there anything else you can tell me? Something that might point me in the right direction?"

"There may be one thing I can try. We're a little lucky that it's a potion-enhanced curse. That might give us a clue." Percival tapped the vial again, and magic enveloped it. This time, a puff of white smoke emerged, with the outline of what appeared to be a town.

"Hm." Percival nodded. "Have your victims been anywhere near Middleburg recently?"

Bev blinked. "Middleburg? Why?"

"Something about this blood has been there in the past week," he said. "Either the potion ingredients used to cast the curse, or the potion itself. I'd wager if you headed to town, you might be able to find the person who made it." He peered into the smoke again. "Whoever they were…they've got some skill with potion-making."

Bev bit her lip. "Hendry's going to be *insufferable*."

Chapter Thirteen

"I knew it."

Hendry, Ida, and Bev sat in the mayor's office, as Bev told them what she'd learned from Percival. She, of course, left out the particulars of *where* she'd had the conversation, but Hendry's knowing nod seemed to indicate she understood. If Ida had questions, they were long forgotten when Bev mentioned the implication of Middleburg.

"Then it's sabotage," Ida said. "Those dastardly Middleburg people. How dare they try to steal our festival again?"

"He didn't say it was someone from Middleburg, just that the ingredients for the potion the curse-caster took were from there," Bev said, trying to be calm before the other two found pitchforks and marched all the way to the other town. "It makes sense. After all, there's not much magic here in Pigsend."

"Sounds like there's lots of magic around Pigsend," Ida said, smiling at Bev. "Where is this person again?"

"There was also a rather large influx of magic around the solstice, which triggered more than a few people's magic," Bev continued, ignoring Ida's question. "It's not a stretch to think someone wanted that magic back. Maybe they were practicing and accidentally cursed the victims."

"That's unlikely, considering Etheldra was in her kitchen," Hendry said. "No, they were targeted. I don't think it was an accident that all three were alone." She inhaled, looking victorious. "I think the best next step is to pay Miranda a visit."

"Miranda Twinsly?" Bev said. "The Middleburg mayor? Why?"

"She *ought* to know there's magical mischief afoot in her own town. Especially if she's the one behind it." Hendry's smile curled like she was a cat about to pounce. "We confront her, make her spill her guts, then once everyone is awake, we'll hand her over to the nearest soldier."

"Then it's settled," Ida said. "We're all going to Middleburg."

"We?" Bev blinked. "Who's we? I've got to get

back to the inn."

"The inn will be fine," Ida said. "Vellora can look after it while we're gone. And it's not that far, anyway. An hour up the road by wagon, right? We go, bang on some doors, threaten some people, get some answers, we're home before dinner."

"I can't," Bev said. "I've spent all morning away from the inn. I have to get my bread in the oven, and—"

"*Think* of poor Etheldra," Hendry said with a sad shake of her head. "And Trent and Herman. They need you, Bev. We've got to get answers, don't we? And clearly, they're in Middleburg. So the logical next step is…"

~

The next thing Bev knew, she was sitting in Ida's wagon, rocking slowly as they made their way to Middleburg. Bev spun around, blinking wildly as she tried to piece together how she'd ended up here from Hendry's office. The mayor sat in the front beside Ida, talking in low tones.

"That's real nice, Hendry," Bev said with a growl, rubbing her face. "Using your magic on me like that. What about the inn?"

"Re-*lax*," Ida said. "Lillie said she'd tend to your bread and get dinner out for you. Allen said he'd check any guests in and get them settled. They were both very keen to let you get out of Pigsend for a bit."

Bev opened and closed her mouth. If there was anyone in town Bev would trust to keep an eye on things, it was Lillie and Allen. "Oh."

"Not as if you've got much space for customers," Hendry said, watching the dirt road before them. "What with Howser and the three victims taking up half your rooms."

That was certainly true, but Bev didn't like the idea of being gone for dinner. Based on the sun in the sky, that was looking like a real possibility. "How far until Middleburg?"

"Half-hour, maybe," Ida said. "Relax, Bev. Enjoy the ride."

Bev was still agitated that she'd been bamboozled into coming along, but eventually, the gentle motion of the wagon relaxed the tension in her body, and she sat back, watching the farmland pass slowly by. They were well out of Pigsend now, and all around were rolling hills, some farms and orchards—green everywhere the eye could see. A cool breeze ruffled the grasses, sending waves along the landscape. They rolled past livestock pens filled with plump cows and bleating goats standing around small ponds, a field of late summer corn that was ready to be harvested, and an orchard of apple trees with dots of red and green in the branches.

"Beautiful out here, isn't it?" Hendry said, perhaps reading Bev's mind. "I swear, we don't leave Pigsend enough. Not as if we have the chance to, but..."

"You should go with us on meat deliveries," Ida said. "Vellora and I are out this way all the time."

"I'll pass, thanks," Hendry said with a scowl. "I'm not a fan of *livestock*."

Bev chuckled as a pair of black and white cows ambled up to the roadside fence. They turned their heads to watch the wagon go by, chewing slowly.

"So what's our plan when we get to Middleburg?" Bev asked, for lack of anything else to say.

"First, we're going to speak with Miranda," Hendry said. "See what she knows about this magical nonsense in her town."

"You're going to use your magic on her, right?" Ida said.

Hendry shifted, clearly not comfortable talking about it. "She's wise to my ways, so we'll have to be sneaky about it. But I can try."

"And if she knows nothing?" Bev asked.

"I've got a few more people to check with," Hendry said. "Don't worry, Bev. We're not dragging you all the way to Middleburg for nothing."

Bev certainly didn't understand why her presence was necessary, but as the town came into view in the distance, she wasn't too unhappy at the change of pace. Compared to Pigsend, Middleburg was a large town, with two- and three-story buildings arranged in a grid, cobblestone streets, and many more people walking those streets. The spacious farmlands had turned into townhouses, three or four smashed together on a single block. Laundry hung in windows above storefronts, and even though there wasn't a cow or sheep to be seen, a distinct odor permeated the air.

"Have you been here before?" Ida asked Bev.

"It's been a long time," Bev said. Truly, she had no reason to visit Middleburg, as anything she might need that wasn't found in Pigsend was usually brought to her by traveling merchants. As the wagon moved through the town, she remembered exactly why it hadn't been top of her priority list to come on a social visit. Everyone looked grumpy and miserable, and a pair of gentlemen almost got into a shoving match after running into each other on the street.

"And Miranda's proud to be mayor of this place?" Hendry said with a satisfied smile. "To each their own, I suppose."

They kept riding through town, passing not one but two inns twice the size of the Weary Dragon. The front doors were open, and Bev found herself curious about what was going on inside. Did the innkeepers there take as much pride as Bev did in dinner and breadmaking?

"As if they could put on a warm and welcoming Harvest Festival," Ida said to Hendry. "Where would they put all the people? Goodness, they barely have enough space for the population they have."

Bev couldn't help but agree. She'd often thought Middleburg might be the better place for the festival, as they boasted more available rooms. But it did seem awfully crowded here, as opposed to the spaciousness of Pigsend. And the hour-long trek wasn't that bad for those coming and going.

"There's the town hall," Hendry said, pointing to a spire visible over the top of a row of townhouses. "Gaudy, awful thing."

They turned the corner onto what was clearly a main street, as it was a bit wider than the one they'd been on before. There were more businesses than houses here, and Bev counted at least seven on each side, everything from apothecaries to cobblers to milliners to butchers. Even a baker, with sweets so intricate they'd rival Lillie's best creations, had a place here. The locals wore fine clothes—nicer dresses and pants that hadn't ever seen a speck of farm dirt—and sported fancy hats with feathers and shiny boots.

"Where should I leave the wagon?" Ida asked, looking around. "I don't think it's safe to tie it up."

"That's why there are three of us," Hendry said. "Ida, you stay with the wagon. Bev and I will go inside to chat with Miranda."

Ida didn't seem to love her assignment but didn't argue with Hendry about it. Bev climbed off the back, stretching her legs and back after sitting for so long. It felt odd to be on cobblestone streets, to hear the clatter of wheels usually softened by dirt roads. And the odor, while less intense here, was still present, wrinkling Bev's nose.

"We don't have all day, Bev." Hendry was already halfway up the stone steps to the large town hall building. "Come along."

Bev came to her senses and followed, walking behind Hendry through the tall wooden doors. Inside, there was a distinct echo from all the stone in the walls and floors, muffled by beautifully ornate carpets. Paintings of severe-looking individuals, past mayors of Middleburg, hung on the walls, glaring down at Bev as they walked the hall. The doors, too, all had placards naming an office of some kind or another.

Assistant Farming Liaison

Official Middleburg Records Keeper

"Miranda did say she had lots of staff," Bev said, looking around. "But is all this really necessary?"

"Oh, who knows? Sometimes people like bureaucracy for bureaucracy's sake," Hendry said. "Me, I prefer a slimmed-down administration. Keeps things from getting out of hand. And I know exactly what's going on at all times." She gestured to a door bearing the placard *Assistant to the Official Middleburg Records Keeper.* "What does that even mean? Why do you need an *assistant*? Why not have a single person?"

Bev didn't have an answer, but clearly, if all these people were as busy as they looked, their jobs were necessary. "Where's Miranda's office?"

"Down this way, I—" She stopped short, her eyes widening.

Bev followed her gaze and her breath caught in her throat. Karolina Hunter, a queen's soldier who'd caused the sinkholes in town, stood five paces from them, discussing something quietly with Miranda Twinsly. Neither one noticed Bev or Hendry, and before they could, Hendry grabbed Bev and yanked her into a nearby empty office.

"What are you doing?" Bev asked.

"I want to hear this," Hendry said. "Now hush."

The mayor dashed around the office for a moment until she found two glass cups sitting on the other side of the desk. She handed one to Bev then pressed the other to the door, leaning her ear up against it. Confused, but trusting the mayor, Bev followed suit. Soon the sound of Karolina and Miranda's voices echoed through the glass.

"…going to need more information than that," Karolina said.

"I'm working on it," Miranda said. "Just give me more time."

"That's one thing I don't have, Miranda."

"I know, I know. I'll have something for you by the end of the week, I'm sure."

"Tomorrow. Or I'm taking matters into my own hands."

Bev held her breath, but there was no more to the conversation. She lowered the glass and looked at Hendry, who frowned.

"What was that about?"

"I don't know," Hendry said. "But let's go find out."

Bev had to hope Karolina had moved on from causing sinkholes in unsuspecting towns, especially since she and Miranda were on the same page about whatever they were discussing. But her overall job—the reason for stopping the magic in town—had been to seek out a powerful magical object. Was she still looking for that? And if so, what did that have to do with Miranda Twinsly?

Hendry knew exactly where she was going and marched right up to the open doors proclaiming the mayor's office. A mousey-looking man sat out front scribbling on a piece of paper, and looked up when Hendry and Bev walked in.

"Do you have an appointment?" he asked.

"Mayors don't need appointments," Hendry said, her voice carrying. "Is she in?"

The assistant eyed her. "You're a mayor? Of which town?"

Hendry glowered. "My name is Jo Hendry, and I'm the mayor of Pigsend."

"Mm. Pigsend." He checked the book. "No,

don't have you on the list today. The mayor is quite busy. We may have a small opening tomorrow morning if you'd like to come back."

"No, I'd like to see her now," Hendry said.

"I'm afraid that's not possible. You'll have to come back tomorrow."

Back and forth they went, and Bev got the distinct impression Hendry was starting to use her magic on the unsuspecting assistant. But even her impressive powers of persuasion were no match for the man, who stared back at her with an unwavering glint in his eye. Miranda seemed to have guessed Hendry might try something like this and had hired an assistant impermeable to Hendry's persuasive ways on the off chance the Pigsend mayor came to town.

"*Fine*, we'll come back tomorrow," Hendry huffed, her face red from arguing. "But be sure to tell Miranda we'll be here *first thing* and to *not* be late."

Bev followed Hendry out the door, surprised that the mayor's insistence hadn't worked. "What do we do now? Go back to Pigsend?"

"No," Hendry said with a knowing smile. "We're going to find the mayor ourselves and have a chat with her. If she thinks she can hide from me, she's got another think coming."

"I saw Karolina Hunter come out," Ida said, a

little breathlessly. "What in the world is she doing here?"

"Plotting with Miranda, it appears," Hendry said, telling Ida about what they'd heard. "Our next move is to find Miranda somewhere in this sorry excuse for a town and confront her directly."

"Where are we going to find her?" Bev asked. "And how do you know so much about Middleburg anyway?"

"Bev, clearly, I do research on all my opponents," Hendry said with a hearty roll of her eyes. "That includes Miranda Twinsly and the entire town of Middleburg." She scanned the large main square and pointed to a small tavern on the other side. "There. I know for a fact she eats dinner there most every night. I say we head over and stake out the place until we see her."

"Good. I'm starving," Ida muttered, rubbing her belly.

Bev, however, didn't love that idea. She nodded toward the apothecary on the other side of the square. "I'm going to go over there and ask around. If the ingredients were sourced here, maybe they came from that shop."

"Or we could wait for Miranda," Hendry said. "And she'll tell us everything we need to know."

"Just on the off chance she doesn't," Bev said with a tap of her nose. "I'm going to keep looking. You did insist that I come, after all. This is what I do."

"*Fine.*" Hendry let out a heaving sigh. "Ida, you stay here and watch for Miranda. Bev and I will go bother the local tincture-maker."

Chapter Fourteen

The small bell above the door tinkled, and Bev
was hit by the scents of various herbs and plants.
The apothecary, a middle-aged woman with leathery
skin and large eyebrows, looked up as Bev and
Hendry walked in. "What'dya need?"

"Afternoon," Bev said, making like she was
looking around.

Hendry, of course, made no show of trying to
pretend she was there for anything more than to talk
with the apothecary. "Do you deal with any magical
items? Ones that could cause a curse?"

The apothecary barked a laugh. "And be arrested
by the queen's people? Absolutely not."

"Yes, I've seen a few of her folk around town

today," Hendry continued. "Any of them been by to bug you about your tinctures? They do like to do that in our town."

"Yeah, they came by." She sniffed. "What town you from?"

"Pigsend," Bev said. "You might know our local apothecary, Bernard?"

"Yeah, I know him." She turned back to Hendry. "Why are you asking about magic? Are you one of the soldiers? Here to see if I'm doing any sort of trade under the table?"

"Yes, actually," Hendry said with a smile.

The prickle of magic touched Bev's skin, and she chewed her lip.

The apothecary blinked and shook her head, as if she were about to fall asleep.

"What can you tell us about magical comas?" Hendry asked. "And how to cast a curse that will cause someone to fall asleep. What ingredients you'd need to use."

"Nothing." Her words came out slurred. "I know nothing about that. What I did know, I made myself forget. No use in keeping any knowledge that could get me in trouble."

"Right, you don't know," Hendry said. "But I think you might know of someone who *does* know, don't you?"

Slowly, the apothecary nodded. "He's rarely in town, though. Comes through every so often. He deals in magical stuff. Don't know where he gets it, but he's always got someone with a magical item to sell."

Bev blinked. "Is his name Winston?"

"I couldn't tell you for sure. There are three or four that I know of."

"Who's Winston?" Hendry asked. "And why haven't I heard of him?"

"He's, erm… He helps out our downward neighbors," Bev said, unsure how much the Middleburg apothecary would remember of their conversation. "And he's the one Bathilda sells to."

Hendry's eyes lit up in recognition. "I see."

"The lot of them like to do deals at the tavern across the way. Always have something interesting up their sleeves, so I hear. If someone comes to me and asks for a magical something or another, I'll send them over there." She paused, swaying. "Or to Pigsend to see Bernard."

"Bernard doesn't use magic," Bev said.

"He uses more than you'd expect," she replied with a smile. "But that's all I know."

"So you do," Hendry said and cleared her throat. "Come, Bev. It appears all our answers lie at the tavern across the way."

Bev followed her out, glaring at the back of her head. "So you really made me investigate the sinkholes and Harvest Festival and all the other nonsense happening in town when you could just wheedle the truth out of everyone?"

"All that *nonsense* was caused by members of the queen's forces," Hendry said mildly. "What do you think *they* would've done when they'd come to after I'd spelled them?"

"Okay, that's a fair point," Bev said.

"Not only that, but having the truth out of someone's mouth isn't the same as having proof of their crime," Hendry said, her gaze sweeping the town square. "Which is why we're here, trying to get the truth out of Miranda so we can find the proof back in Pigsend."

Bev didn't disagree, but there was something more concerning in her mind. "Have you ever done that to me?"

"Done what?"

"Put me under a spell? Made me tell you everything?" Bev asked.

Hendry turned to purse her lips at Bev. "Please, do say that louder. I don't think Karolina heard you."

Bev nodded. "Point taken. Sorry."

"As a general rule, I don't use that kind of… well, you know. It's dangerous, especially these days. And in a town like Pigsend, where everyone knows who I am, there's only so many times I can put someone under a…well, put someone under like that without the whole town realizing something's up."

That made sense. "So you've never done that to me?"

Hendry clicked her tongue. "Once. When you first arrived in town. I wanted to see if you truly had no memory or if you were playing like you did."

Bev's heart swooped in her chest. "And?"

"And your mind was as empty as a plate of rosemary bread after Etheldra's been through," Hendry said. "And that's the truth. Whatever happened to you, happened very soundly and fully. There are no memories buried in your mind anywhere. At least, none that I could find." She adjusted her shirt. "Come. To the tavern. I'm sure Miranda will be there soon."

~

Bev and Hendry walked into the tavern, which was dark and crowded. It seemed perfect for the kind of underhanded dealing the apothecary said went on here, but not quite so obvious for a mayor to frequent. Unless she, too, dealt in more underhanded things than Bev thought a mayor should.

"Find a table," Hendry said. "Somewhere with a good view of the door."

"Where are you going?" Bev asked.

"To get us food. I'm famished." Hendry reached into her pocket and counted out a few coins and then walked to the tavern bar.

Bev found a table and sat, feeling quite strange

to be served instead of serving. Workers flitted around with trays and plates of food, dropping them off at tables where hungry diners waited. There was no self-serve here, and Bev counted at least five workers besides the tender behind the bar.

"Here." Hendry handed her a bowl. "I doubt it's anywhere as good as ours. And this bread is…" She flung down a few crusty pieces of bread that appeared to have been baked over a day ago. "But it's food."

Hendry's assessment was correct, but it was edible, and Bev was hungry, so she ate as much as she could. She stared forlornly at the stale bread and wished it was her own loaf, fresh from the oven. No wonder the travelers raved about it, if this was what they got everywhere else.

"What do you reckon, Bev?" Hendry asked, sucking down some of the foam atop her beer tankard.

"Hm?"

"About today. About Karolina, the apothecary. Bernard."

"Did you know he dealt with magic?" Bev asked. "That's a silly question. Of course you did."

She nodded. "Nothing too obvious, as that would arouse suspicion. But yes, he does a few things here and there. Where do you think I got the lacquer for the chairs Earl built me?" Her eyes sparkled. "That's why I know he's not behind this.

It's too risky. He makes a tidy business doing things under the table. Any light shines on it, and he's cooked."

That certainly made sense. "Then it's someone out to get him. Or something else."

"Or it's Miranda plotting to ruin our festival," Hendry said. "Honestly, Bev, when you have all this evidence, why are you still looking for an alternate explanation?"

"Because the obvious explanation isn't always the right one," Bev said. "Or it isn't right in the way you were thinking. I know there's something I'm missing."

"Well, why don't we go ask Miranda about it?" Hendry said with a smug smile. "Because she just walked in the door."

Bev followed Hendry's gaze, spotting the Middleburg mayor breezing through the door. She waved hello to a few people, shook some hands, then sat at a table that had been made ready for her. Within seconds of her sitting, there was a full plate of food and a tankard of ale in front of her, and she tucked in.

"Must be nice to be the mayor," Bev said.

"C'mon," Hendry said, throwing her shoulders back and crossing the tavern. Bev kept her distance to remain out of their back-and-forth. Hendry didn't seem to care that she was interrupting Miranda's meal as she walked right up to the table.

"I thought I smelled the stench of Pigsend around here," Miranda said, seemingly unsurprised to see them. "Goodness, Jo, you look absolutely dreadful. Did you walk here or something?"

"The only thing that stinks around here is Middleburg's continued disruption of Pigsend's Harvest Festival," Hendry shot back. "I demand to know what you've done to our townsfolk, and insist you give us a cure immediately."

Miranda sat back, amused. "What in the world are you talking about? I've not been to Pigsend since that awful sham of an election."

"Then someone you sent has," Hendry said. "And I demand to know—"

"There's no need for you to use your magic here," Miranda said, gesturing to the table. "I'll tell you everything you want to know, Jo. Come, come. There's no need for all this hostility."

Hendry and Bev sat, Hendry watching her nemesis suspiciously. "Yeah? Why are you being so nice? Anything to do with Karolina Hunter in your office earlier?"

"Please, I saw you two skulking about," Miranda said evenly. "And yes, it's in pursuit of moving the Harvest Festival. But you can't blame me for taking advantage of a situation."

"What situation is that?" Bev asked.

"You've got three victims in a magical coma," Miranda said, as if that were common knowledge everywhere.

"So it *was* you who did it," Bev said.

"Oh goodness, no." Miranda laughed. "I wouldn't know the first thing about casting curses. But whoever is doing it seems to be doing me a favor."

"How so?" Hendry asked.

"All the queen's people are on edge because there are murmurs and whispers of magical folks coming out of the woodwork. Three people in a magical coma? I think that shows there's someone quite powerful in Pigsend." She crossed her arms over her chest. "And with it being *such* a hotbed of magical activity, it would certainly make sense to move the Harvest Festival to a safer community."

She spoke so plainly, but every word made Bev's blood boil. Hendry, too, looked like she was about to throw a fit. "That's real nice, Miranda. People have been hurt in Pigsend, and all you care about is the Harvest Festival?"

Miranda shrugged. "Don't tell me you wouldn't do the same thing, Jo."

Miranda had Hendry there. "You told Karolina you were going to get something for her." Bev tilted her head. "What was it?"

"Proof, darling. Proof," Miranda said. "Wouldn't it be incredible if the denizens of Middleburg found out what was causing all the magical affliction in Pigsend?"

"And how are you planning to do that?" Hendry asked. "I haven't seen any of your kind skulking about our town."

She sighed. "Well, *unfortunately*, my control over the law enforcement here in Middleburg isn't quite as tight as Mayor Hendry's is over that dear Sheriff Rustin." She looked around. "Where is he, anyway? I didn't think he left your side."

"He's doing his job back in Pigsend," Hendry said. "What do you mean? You can't control your own sheriff?"

She patted Hendry's hand. "Sheriffs, dear, plural. And no, I don't control them. Her Majesty has her eye on Middleburg more than a tiny little town like Pigsend. So…well, I'm working on getting approval for them to come out to Pigsend." She sighed. "*Apparently*, they want Rustin to handle it. Give him a chance to redeem himself or whatever."

Bev was actually happy to hear that. "The apothecary across the street said there was a merchant who comes and goes from here with magical things. We think he might be the one who supplied the goods. Do you know who she might be talking about?"

Miranda took a bite of her meal, seeming to think for a moment. "I like you, Bev, so I'll be straight with you. I don't know who you're referring to, but that doesn't mean they aren't here. There are more than a few businesses in town that deal in that sort of thing, but I don't want to know anything about it."

"And does *Her Majesty* know there's all kinds of illegal buying and selling of magic in this tavern?" Hendry asked. "Because I can't imagine she'd condone such a thing. Funny how you're content to work both sides of the coin."

Twinsly arched her brow. "That's rich, coming from you."

"Can you two have a moment without snapping at each other?" Bev said. "Goodness, you're worse than Trent and Herman. It's a shame you didn't get zapped by the curse."

That seemed to chasten them both.

"Now," Bev said, adjusting her tunic, "is there *anything* you can tell us about this, Miranda?"

"Until I'm allowed to send my people to Pigsend, no," she said. "But if I were you, I might start asking questions of that apothecary. If you're looking for someone who makes magical potions, I daresay you shouldn't look farther than him."

~

Bev and Hendry left the tavern after that, and Bev was surprised to see pink clouds streaking the sky above. It was much later than she'd thought, but the dark tavern didn't have many windows.

"Well, this has been a fruitless trip," Hendry said as they walked up to Ida. "We've discovered nothing new that will help us."

"Bernard?" Bev suggested.

"If Bernard had something to share, he would have," Hendry said wearily. "He's the one who's trying to save the folks, remember?"

"Yes, but—"

"Bernard isn't our culprit," Hendry said. "And, *annoyingly*, it appears that Middleburg is the just the source of the ingredients. If Miranda says she doesn't know who did it, I believe her." Hendry sniffed. "Doesn't mean I like that she's taking advantage of our misery, but clearly, we need to look elsewhere for our guilty party."

"So…" Bev tried hard not to be smug. "I was right?"

"Nobody likes a know-it-all," Hendry snapped. "Come on. It's getting late. I don't want to spend a second more in this town than we have to."

"But I'm *hungry*," Ida whined. "And it's so long until we get back. You two didn't bring me a piece of bread or anything like that from the tavern?"

"It's not that good," Bev said.

Ida whined again, and Bev took pity on her friend. The bakery across the street was closed, so the only option was to go back to the tavern and get something Ida could eat on the road. Even in the few minutes she'd been gone, the tavern had grown even more crowded as people were eager to eat and socialize. Miranda had already made her escape, and three more people had taken her table.

Bev walked up to the bar, hoping to flag down the tender to get a piece of bread, at least, but they were moving too quickly to stop and speak with her. While she waited, she cast her gaze around the tavern, looking for anyone suspicious.

Her gaze landed on a very familiar face, and Bev's heart dropped to her stomach. "Etheldra?"

The woman staring back at her was almost the spitting image of the tea shop owner. But no, there were small differences. Something in the eyes, a slightly larger nose. Hair that fell a different way. Still, the resemblance was so uncanny, Bev had no choice but to blurt out the woman's name.

"Sherry?"

Chapter Fifteen

The woman took a step back, surprise obvious on her face. She looked around for a moment, perhaps searching for an exit, before shaking her head. "You must be mistaken. My name is Penny."

But Bev was sure she wasn't mistaken. "I'm, erm…well, I'm friends with your sister. What are you doing in Middleburg?"

The woman's cheeks grew pink. "You're wrong. I have no sister. My name is Penny Howser, I—"

"Penny, what are you doing?" Another woman wearing the same dress as Sherry came up to her. "I've got a table over there that hasn't been served yet."

"Right, sorry. Got distracted by—" Sherry ran

her hand down the front of her dress, which Bev realized was an apron.

"Do you work here?" Bev asked.

"No, erm, yes, but…" Sherry's face grew blotchy as she turned. "Bye."

She bustled away, disappearing into the kitchen for a moment before reappearing with a tray of ale tankards. She purposefully avoided Bev's gaze as she marched to a table in the back, placing the drinks on the table. Then she scurried back to the kitchen again and didn't emerge.

"What in the *world*?" Bev said. So much for marrying a wealthy sugar merchant or whatever else Trent and Herman had said. If only they'd known the girl of their dreams was serving beer at a tavern in nearby Middleburg.

Or had they? It seemed almost far-fetched that Etheldra's sister and Herman and Trent's long-lost love could've been here in Middleburg this whole time and the news hadn't reached them.

"Wait…" Bev started. Had she said Penny *Howser*?

Bev took a step toward the kitchen, intending to ask more questions, when she felt a strong hand on her arm. Ida wore a look of frustration. "Hendry says if we don't leave in the next five minutes, she's going to go without us. I suppose I can survive an hour until we get home to eat."

Bev hesitated, debating if she should tell Ida

what she'd seen. In the end, Bev decided to keep this revelation to herself until she knew more. And as luck would have it, she might have someone who could answer her burning questions sleeping at her inn.

~

Bev couldn't unstick the short conversation with Sherry from her mind, and barely listened to Hendry and Ida complain about Miranda, Middleburg, and everything that was going wrong in Pigsend. While it was entirely possible for Bev to take her own wagon back to Middleburg tomorrow and demand answers, somehow she got the feeling Sherry wouldn't come out with it.

It was hard to believe a tavern barmaid would be capable of cursing her own sister and former lovers, but it wasn't out of the realm of possibility. After all, Etheldra had a scant amount of magic, though it was limited to combining herbs and plants.

Not to mention…Howser wasn't the most common of names, but it wasn't uncommon. So it was possible that Penny not only looked identical to Etheldra, but also happened to share Doc Howser's last name.

It was also possible Biscuit could start talking.

Still, as much as she felt Sherry could be connected, she was having a hard time understanding *why* Sherry might attack the three. Sibling rivalry could've explained Etheldra, of course, but Sherry had been the one to break Trent and Herman's hearts. Why add insult to injury by cursing them?

"Bev, you've been awfully quiet," Ida said, breaking Bev from her thoughts. "Tell me you've got some new idea you want to pursue."

Once again, Bev demurred on sharing her discovery of Etheldra's sister. "I still think it's fishy Bernard didn't tell us about the magical tinctures he makes."

"Why would he tell me something I already know?" Hendry shot back. "It's not Bernard, I can tell you that."

"Then why didn't he tell *me*?" Bev said. "I think it's worth asking him what else he was making for Etheldra, Herman, and Trent. Maybe there was a mixup in the ingredients. Maybe he's been working himself to the bone to try to undo what he did."

"But wouldn't you have found that?" Ida asked. "Or Biscuit?"

Bev nodded.

"Besides that, didn't your…friend down below say definitively it was a curse?" Hendry said.

"Yes." Bev sighed. "Someone made a potion to get enough magic to cast a curse."

"Maybe Bernard made it, gave it to someone, and he feels guilty about what his potion has done," Ida said.

"I think he would've told us," Hendry said. "I

think the better course of action is to ask ourselves *why* these three were targeted."

"Maybe it's someone from Middleburg working without Miranda's knowledge," Ida said. "I don't think it's coincidence that the three people targeted were the winners of Harvest Festival contests."

"Maybe it is Sherry," Hendry said, glancing at the moon.

Bev almost fell off the wagon. "Why do you say that?"

"Well, last I checked, she's set to inherit everything from our three victims," Hendry said.

Bev almost stood up in the wagon, incredulous. "And you didn't think that was important to share? Hendry, that's *motive*."

"Oh, please. No one's seen Sherry in ages," Hendry said. "Besides that, last I heard, she was living the high life on the coast, married to a dye merchant. I doubt she has any interest in two dusty farms and a tea shop."

But if she was a tavern wench, she might want to inherit the property to line her own threadbare pockets. Still, Bev kept quiet. She didn't want to feed the grapevine in Pigsend anymore than it already had been. Not until she confronted Doc Howser and Bernard and got some honest answers out of them.

The moon was high overhead when the wagon rolled back into Pigsend, and Bev inhaled deeply, grateful to be home. She bade farewell to Hendry and Ida then walked into the inn, greeted by a dimly lit front room. Lillie sat in one of the chairs, reading a book and twirling one of her curls. Biscuit was snoozing at her feet, his snores a welcome sound after the long day.

"You're back!" Lillie said, rousing Biscuit.

The laelaps scurried over to Bev, tail wagging, and she knelt to pet him.

"How did it go?" Bev asked.

"You've got a couple of folks upstairs," Lillie said. "Dinner was all right. I—erm, well, it's been a while since I've baked anything other than sweets, but I think I did okay. The bread was divine, but that was all you, I think." She beamed. "Just the usuals for dinner. I made Earl eat, too. But the poor dear looks absolutely beside himself." She crossed her arms over her chest. "Did you find out anything?"

"Yes and no," Bev said. "But it's been a long day. I think I'm going to turn in. Thank you so much for keeping an eye on things."

"Anything for you, Bev," Lillie said with a loud yawn. "Yes, I think going to bed is a great idea."

Bev saw her out then went to check on things in the kitchen. Every dish was already clean and ready for tomorrow, but Bev still had to make her dough so it could sit in the root cellar overnight. Although she was grateful for Lillie's care of her beloved inn, she was selfishly glad the pobyd had left the breadmaking to Bev. Especially so close to the Harvest Festival, Bev wanted as much practice as she could get.

As soon as she finished her last bit of kneading, the front door opened. Bev peered out from the kitchen, and her pulse skipped when she saw Doc Howser wearily crossing the front room, headed for the stairs.

"Hey," Bev said, rushing out to greet him before he disappeared. "Did you eat? I'm not sure Lillie saved you a plate."

"Yes, I popped by earlier with Bernard." He looked even more tired and old than he had before, and Bev wondered if Earl wasn't the only one not sleeping up there. "I heard you were in Middleburg today."

Bev nodded, watching him carefully. "We were looking for answers about the magical coma."

"Did you find any?"

Bev shook her head. "Came back with more questions."

"Wouldn't think you would find much there. Middleburg is…well, there are lots of people, but since the queen—"

"I saw Sherry," Bev blurted before she could stop herself.

Howser's eyes widened, and he made no attempt to hide his emotions. "You…did?"

"She said she wasn't Etheldra's sister," Bev said. "But they're the spitting image of each other. And she said her name was…" She paused, watching him closely. "She said her name was Penny Howser. I didn't check for a wedding ring, but…"

The good doctor wasn't wearing one, either, but the look on his face was telling enough. "I see. Well, I'm sure you have some questions."

"Why didn't you tell me?" Bev asked.

"Because, like most things in life, it's quite complicated. And Penny—Sherry—was adamant that her presence in Middleburg remain a secret from the folks in Pigsend."

"Yet three people who are connected to her are upstairs, stuck in a magical coma," Bev replied. "You can imagine why I find that suspicious."

He sighed, crossing the room and sitting down on one of the hearthside chairs, offering her the other one. She joined him, grateful she wouldn't have to cajole the truth out of him. She didn't have the energy to be clever about it.

Howser thought for a moment before he spoke. "About three years ago, I was staying in a nice little village called Chelseaville. It's a very small town, like Pigsend, but they were hit hard by dragon pox. About three-quarters of the town was sick with it, and the town was practically shut down for at least a month." He paused. "Sherry had moved there forty years ago and built a nice life for herself selling honey and tending to her bees under the name Penny Woodson. She also happened to have the only spare room in town." He paused again. "She didn't tell me who she was, of course, but I recognized her immediately."

"Why did she change her name?" Bev asked. "Why all the secrecy? Etheldra says they hadn't written in forty years."

"They had a fraught relationship. You know Etheldra. She can be…" He cleared his throat. "And she was even worse to her younger sister." He gave Bev a half smile. "And as I understand it, neither Trent nor Herman were very good at taking no for an answer. Penny—Sherry—got tired of having to tell them she wasn't interested in either of them. Thought a fresh start in a new town was the ticket."

"But then you arrived," Bev said.

He smiled. "Sherry had already taken ill in her youth and was immune, so I asked her to assist me. Working together over those weeks, sharing meals and memories of our youth in Pigsend…well…" His grin widened, and Bev saw the spark of new love in his old eyes. "Unfortunately, Chelseaville is on the very edge of my practice area, so the logistics of coming and going would be difficult. I convinced her to move to my home in Middleburg. When I'm not, erm, in Pigsend, she travels and assists me."

"And when you are in Pigsend, she's serving drinks?"

"Something to keep her busy," he said. "She unfortunately had to give up her beloved bees when she moved."

"I see." Bev rubbed her hands together. "And you don't think it's…suspicious that Herman, Trent, and Etheldra all succumbed to this magical coma? Hendry tells me Sherry's in line to inherit their property."

"Is she?" That certainly looked like news to Howser. "I suppose after all this time, both Trent and Herman still can't take no for an answer."

"I didn't confront her about this," Bev said. "Because I wanted to speak with you first. I can understand why Sherry wanted to keep her life a secret from everyone else, but you also have to see how and why it looks like she's the guilty party."

Howser shook his head. "I know what it looks like, but I promise you, Penny isn't involved. She washed her hands of Pigsend a long time ago. Why would she want to hurt anyone here when she's content in her current life?"

~

Bev spent most of the night debating how and when she'd return to Middleburg to speak with Sherry. Before she made the trip, though, she wanted to confirm what Hendry had told her about the inheritance. So, after seeing her guests off with a few of Allen's breakfast biscuits, Bev made her way to the Pigsend town square to speak with Max. The librarian was also the town record-keeper, and Bev had to assume that meant any wills or things like that. If Sherry was still the coma patients' beneficiary, Bev would have some more questions for Howser about his new bride.

Max was at his desk, scribbling in a journal, and greeted Bev warmly. "Hey, there, Bev! Missed you last night. I hear you were in Middleburg. Did you find our culprit?"

"Maybe," Bev said, a little evasively. "I wanted to ask if you knew where I could find any sort of wills or inheritance documents."

"For Trent, Herman, and Etheldra?" Max chuckled. "Once again, Bev, you and I are on the same wavelength. Although they're not *dead,* per se, some of the old laws around magical comas haven't been updated quite yet, so one could argue that their present state and lack of cure means their property could go to someone else."

Bev bit her lip. "So who would get it?"

"Surprisingly, both Trent *and* Herman have left their farms to the same person," Max said. "Sherry Dawes."

"You don't say." Bev pretended to look surprised. "Is that Etheldra's sister?"

"Yes. The trio were entangled once upon a time." He shook his head. "It was the gossip of the town when it happened. A girl dated Herman, then dated Trent, then skipped out. And for Herman *and*

Trent to both leave their farms to her? That's true love."

"Yeah." If only they'd known. "So you say if Sherry knew about their present state, she could… well, she could inherit their land?"

"It would take some arguing in front of a judge, and one who doesn't know much about magical curses, which is most of them now, I'd wager. But I believe she could be successful."

"What about Etheldra's shop?" Bev asked.

"Oh, that, actually, I updated," he said.

"Because she's married to Earl, right?"

"No, no. Etheldra was *insistent* that not be the case," he said. "She wanted her things to remain hers and Earl's to remain his. But I suppose when one reaches a certain age, that's the way of things."

"So who gets the shop?" Bev pressed.

"Shasta Brewer," he said. "It's part of the agreement they signed a few weeks ago. Shasta pays Etheldra a certain amount of her wages to cover the mortgage. When the debt is satisfied, Shasta becomes the full owner. Or should Etheldra pass away or become incapacitated, the shop goes to Shasta."

Bev looked out the window. From this angle, she could see the awning over the tea shop. "Do you think Shasta might've put Etheldra in a coma to hasten the transfer?"

"I doubt it," he said. "And why attack Trent and

Herman?"

That was the question of the week. "Thank you, Max. I appreciate you looking into this for me."

"Anything to help out the resident sleuth." He snapped his fingers. "That reminds me, I did get a new book in. Erm, it might not have come via the most *legal* of methods, but since you're interested in those things, maybe you'd like to see it?"

"Sure," Bev said.

"Give me one moment."

He turned to disappear into the back, and Bev tapped her fingers on the counter. Her original theory about the Brewer twins as scheming to discredit one employer and incapacitate another still felt far-fetched, but it certainly merited investigating further. Maybe she could bring Biscuit over, and he could—

Thump.

Bev turned toward the back. "Max? Are you all right?"

When there was no answer, Bev hurried around the counter to the back. Her heart sank to her stomach when she found Max, staring at the sky, facing up, not moving.

"Not again."

Chapter Sixteen

While Bev was obviously concerned for Max's health and well-being, the more pressing concern in her mind was how very off-pattern this attack was. Max had no connection to the Harvest Festival at all, and he obviously hadn't known anything about Sherry other than being the holder of records. But Bev *did* find a tincture vial from Bernard as she searched Max's office. It was off to the side, though, not on him.

She didn't bring that up immediately, as Hendry had been adamant Bernard wasn't the culprit. But the apothecary was the only thread left connecting the four victims.

But to what end? To expose Bernard as a magic-wielding apothecary, making and selling illegal potions? Could Gerry have orchestrated something from all the way down in Lower Pigsend? Or did Bernard have another nemesis he didn't know about?

Bev pondered these questions as she gathered with Hendry and Ida in Hendry's office to discuss the latest development. Max had been moved to the inn, and Bev had fashioned him a comfortable spot on the floor with Trent and Herman. All three had the same ashen complexion, and none of them breathed.

"I'm starting to get worried," Ida said. "What if they are random attacks? Someone who's decided to terrorize the town for no reason."

"Tell me again exactly what happened," Hendry said to Bev.

She recounted every detail, from speaking with Max about Sherry's inheritance to him disappearing into his office in the back to get a book. Said book was under his arm, but there didn't seem to be any remnants of magic on it (and Biscuit had checked). There *was*, however, an open window in Max's office, though Bev hadn't seen anyone when she'd found Max.

"But why Max? Why now?" Ida asked.

"I don't know," Bev said, shaking her head. "I really don't know."

"I tell you what we need to do now," Hendry

said, after a moment. "I think we need some more of that crumble."

Ida and Bev stared at her like she had two heads. "I'm sorry, what?" Bev said.

"That crumble. The one with iron you gave to everyone at the solstice," Hendry said. "If the person responsible is shooting magic at everyone, wouldn't a bit of iron in the system act as a shield?"

It was logical, but Bev didn't know exactly how protective it would be. Percival hadn't suggested it as a possible cure to the curse. "I…suppose…"

"Then it's settled," Hendry said. "As soon as news spreads about Max, there's going to be someone demanding a town meeting. We can serve it there."

"I can't guarantee that it'll work," Bev said. "And rhubarb is out of season, so—"

"Then apple. Whatever you like. Throw some oats on it as well and make it a crisp, for some variety," Hendry said. "And cinnamon. That actually sounds delicious." She headed to the door. "Chop, chop, Bev. I'm sure we'll be meeting this evening."

~

Without anything else to offer, Bev resigned herself to making another iron-infused baked good to share with the town. She still had the satchel of nails and willow bark she'd cooked the first crumble with buried in a drawer. She considered she probably didn't need the willow this time, as no one was feeling ill, but the iron nails would be able to infuse their magic-fighting properties into the final dish.

She didn't have anything other than flour to make it with, so she headed across the street to the bakers first to see what she could borrow. Lillie was icing a multi-tiered cake, her tongue sticking out as she piped intricate designs on the top. Allen was mixing a pastry dough of some kind, his face smeared with flour.

"Apples?" Lillie and Allen shared a look. "No, we're fresh out. But I'm sure the farmers' market has some."

"That's my next stop," Bev said.

"What are you making?" Lillie asked.

Bev told her of Hendry's request, and Lillie quirked a brow. "Erm. I'm not sure that's going to work. It might, but... Curses are pretty potent things, you know? You need a lot of magic to make one. Eating some iron isn't going to stop it, I don't think."

"It might not be about stopping it," Allen said, putting down the bowl. "Maybe Hendry's worried the town's going to panic. We do tend to get nervous when there's magic around. Even if they think only it's protective, that might help keep everyone's nerves steady."

"I hadn't even considered that," Bev said. "But that does sound like something Hendry would do."

"Right down to putting the onus on *you* to make something," Lillie said with a chuckle.

"Suppose it's my lot in life," Bev replied with a weary sigh. "Any ideas how I could mask the iron taste? Even if I get tart apples, I'm not sure they'll do the trick."

"Oh, we got a large crate of cranberries in from the north," Lillie said, her face lighting up. "I wanted to try some cranberry-based pastries this fall. Some breads and compotes, you know? We have so many, though. More than I'm sure I could use." She thumbed toward the back. "Take as many as you like."

Bev had used cranberries with pork whenever she could snag a few from Allen, but she'd never used them in a baked good. When cooked, they burst and exuded a beautifully tart red syrup. Mixed with apples and cinnamon, it would certainly be delicious.

With the carton of cranberries obtained, Bev hooked Sin up to the wagon and headed to the market for said apples. Her heart hurt as she passed Herman's farm, though his pumpkins were still looking healthy and ripe despite the lack of care given to them over the past few days.

"We'll get you awake soon, Herman," Bev muttered. "And you can enter your pumpkins in the festival, and everything will be right."

When she arrived at the market, everyone there

was on edge. Alice Estrich had a large staff by her side and grabbed it nervously as Bev walked up.

"Is it you, Bev?" she asked.

"Who else would it be?" Bev asked.

"Not sure if whoever's cursing people all over town is showing up dressed as someone they knew," she said, slowly lowering the staff.

Bev didn't have the heart to tell her that a wooden staff was *probably* no match for whoever was cursing people. "Does anyone have any apples today?"

"I think Grant Klose does," she said, nodding to a stall down the way. "Any news? I hear we've got a town meeting tonight."

That was fast. "Yeah, I heard that, too," Bev said. "Max was attacked this morning."

She shook her head. "Two farmers, the tea shop owner, now the librarian. Someone's got it out for everyone in Pigsend."

"It certainly appears that way," Bev said. Then, remembering what Allen had said, she added, "I'm making an apple cranberry crisp infused with iron. Hendry thinks that might be enough to keep the curse at bay."

Alice's eyes lit up. "You think? Oh, Bev. You're such a saint. I was thinking about skipping the town meeting, but if you're bringing that, I'll be there for sure."

Bev promised she'd save Alice a bowlful then

walked down to Grant Klose's stall. The farmer, too, was nervous as Bev approached, but seemed to relax when she announced her intentions.

"Can't be too careful," he said, picking up the bushel of apples.

"You haven't seen anything suspicious, have you?" Bev asked.

He shook his head. "But I was talking with Eldred Nest the other day. He's insistent he's seen someone come out of the ground on repeated occasions."

"He's off his rocker."

Bev jumped at the gravelly voice beside her. Officer Nog, covered in potions to make him look more human than goblin, took the bushels Bev was about to buy and held them away from her.

"These mine?" he asked.

"Er, sure. Bev, have you met Gon?" Grant asked. "He moved to town a few weeks ago, he said."

Gon? Certainly not taking great lengths to hide his name. "We're well acquainted," Bev said with a thin smile. "How are you today, erm, *Gon?*"

"Better once I get on my way," he snarled. "And you tell that Eldred Nest that he needs to quit spouting nonsense. There's no need to be scaring people about underground moles and whatnot."

Bev could certainly understand why Nog was eager to quell that rumor. "I agree," she said. "We've got enough to worry about."

Grant shrugged. "I don't think anyone can tell Eldred anything. He's got a mind of his own, you know? Is that going to be all, Gon?"

Nog paid him then moved on to the next stall to fill his wagon. Grant had another bushel of apples for Bev, and she paid him quickly and put them in her own wagon. Nog was talking with Alice, who eyed him warily but still sold him some potatoes.

Bev approached as Nog was loading the last of his produce onto the wagon. "Everything all right where you are?"

He grunted. "Fine. Nothing to report."

"Eldred's talk of—"

"Just talk, nothing more." Even though he was covered in magic, his cheeks still reddened. "Nothing to say to you."

"You are, of course, aware of the attacks that have been happening," Bev said, glancing around. "Four people have gone into a magical coma."

"Eh. Maybe I heard something. What about it?"

"Gerry hasn't been allowed to the surface lately, right?" Bev said.

Nog eyed her. "Why?"

"Because it's starting to look like someone's framing his brother," Bev said. "And the only person who'd want to do that is—"

"It sounds like you should be having this conversation with *him,* then," Nog said, climbing onto the wagon. "I'm no longer in charge of keeping track of people. I get the food and deliver the food."

Bev cleared her throat. "What about Winston?"

"What about him?"

"Is he local?" Bev asked. "Hanging around somewhere I could speak with him?"

"He's here and there. We don't get to control him, either." He snapped the reins. "Now, if you'll excuse me…"

Nog goaded his mule on, and Bev had to wonder if the creature wasn't some other magical beast of burden under disguise. Sin brayed and stamped her foot, a signal to Bev that the old mule was getting annoyed with being out of her stall, so Bev left it alone and headed back to the inn.

~

"Biscuit," Bev said when she walked through the door. "Do you recall where the opening to Lower Pigsend is—the one Shamus uses, not Merv's house."

Her laelaps sat, listening intently.

"I want to make sure there's no funny business coming from there," Bev said. "I'm going to head over to Eldred's house again and talk with him. It could be nothing, but I have a hunch something fishy's coming out of Lower Pigsend again. While I'm talking with Eldred, go sniff around the entrance, okay? If you scent anything that smells like our four victims, come get me."

She unloaded her fruit and made sure she had

everything she needed. Dinner went in the oven, though she hadn't a clue who was coming, as half of her regular customers were upstairs. The crisp wouldn't take that long to prep and bake, and she wanted to speak with Eldred and make sure he hadn't seen anything.

But as she passed the apothecary shop, she found herself wanting to ask Bernard questions—especially around his side business as an illegal potion maker.

She opened the door, the bell tinkling above, and smiled as Stella greeted her. "What can I do for you today?"

"Is Bernard back there?" Bev asked. "Have a question for him."

"Probably. But he's been biting my head off whenever I bother him, so be careful." She shook her head. "I know he's stressed about all the attacks, and I am, too, but goodness. Don't take it out on me."

Bev found Bernard hard at work again. He still looked as if he hadn't slept, and Bev once again wondered at the source of his guilt.

"Stella, I told you—oh." His face fell. "Don't tell me there's been another victim."

"Not yet," Bev said. "Other than Max, but I assume you already heard."

He shook his head. "So much for the Harvest Festival theory."

"Indeed." Bev rocked on her heels a moment, unsure how to broach the subject. "We went to Middleburg."

He made a noise as he combined two ingredients.

"The local apothecary there told us that if we were in need of a magical potion, we should come to you," Bev said.

Bernard looked up, meeting her gaze for a moment, then back down. "Since it's you, Bev, I won't deny it."

"Did you make magical tinctures for the victims?" Bev asked. "Other than the usual ones you already told me about?"

He straightened, closing his eyes for a moment. "Trent had asked me for a potion to grow his pumpkins. Something undetectable."

"Did you give it to him?"

He cracked a smile. "He got a potion of distilled rosemary and thyme. I'm not about to help someone cheat in the Harvest Festival."

"He might've gotten caught anyway," Bev said. "And Herman?"

"He wanted a potion to spread around his property to keep Trent away," Bernard said. "That I could do. A little mint, a little intention. Spread around the pumpkin patch. It also does well to keep the mice away."

Bev nodded slowly. "Etheldra?"

He cleared his throat. "Well, erm, I don't think I should say. But, erm…" He swallowed hard. "Let's say she wanted a little something for newlywed bliss."

Bev almost choked. "I see."

"At their age, magic was necessary." He blushed and returned to the ingredients, busying himself.

"Max?"

He paused. "That's the thing. Max didn't get anything magical. His tincture was, ironically, for sleep. But it was a mixture of valerian root and lavender. Not a drop of magic in it."

"Were there any of the same ingredients in all four potions?" Bev asked. "Something that could explain—"

"You don't think it was me, do you?" Bernard asked.

"No," Bev said. "But I'm trying to understand if someone's swapped a bad ingredient for a good one, or—"

"I thought you said it was a curse," Bernard said with a frown. "Potions aren't curses."

"No, they're not," Bev said. "But—"

"I think it's a better use of your time to be asking who could cast a curse in town," Bernard said, his face growing red. "Instead of bothering me when I could be working on options to heal the victims. Do you think I cursed them so I could save them?" He gestured to the air. "I haven't slept in days! All I've done is focus on this. And you—"

"I'm not accusing you," Bev said, holding up her hands in surrender. "I'm trying to get to the bottom of things." She paused, glancing at the table. "These magical ingredients…"

"Yes?" His tone was clipped.

"Do you get them from Winston?" Bev asked.

His face twitched, but he nodded. "Yes."

"When is he bringing you another shipment?" Bev asked. "I have some questions for him, too."

Bernard glanced at the clock. "Tonight, actually. I've not had any luck with my usual efforts, so I sent a message to him asking for something a bit more… unique."

"What time are you meeting him?" Bev asked.

"Around eight. During the town meeting, when no one's around."

Bev nodded. "Tell him I want to talk with him, if you will. He could come to the inn, or—"

"I don't think he works like that," Bernard said. "But—"

There was a loud yelp from outside, and Bev recognized Biscuit's bark. She furrowed her brow, opening the door to the apothecary to find Biscuit standing there, tail wagging.

"Did you find something?" Bev asked. The laelaps had continued on when Bev had gone into the apothecary.

Biscuit stood and trotted toward the farmland—

and Bev followed.

She wasn't sure what to expect—Winston or Shamus at the opening to Lower Pigsend, or maybe Biscuit had scented Nog. But as he turned off the road toward Eldred's house, Bev had a sneaking suspicion what Biscuit had seen.

And true enough, Eldred was in his rocking chair, stunned and sleeping, like all the rest. But this time, there was a vial in his hand.

Chapter Seventeen

Bev pulled the vial and sniffed it, detecting the faintest scent of something herbal. She offered it to Biscuit, who sniffed it and wagged his tail. There was magic in this one. Another strike against Bernard? But why, after he knew Bev was looking into him, would he suddenly leave behind a vial?

"What happened?" Bev asked Biscuit.

Biscuit let out a breath, and for the first time, Bev wished her laelaps was able to communicate with words, not barks and whines. But she could tell, based on the still-warm tea sitting next to him, that Eldred hadn't been in this state very long.

"What in the world is going on?" Bev said to herself.

Eldred didn't have enemies. He and Trent got along, so he'd said. The only time Eldred really came to town was for town meetings, where he'd rant and rave about…

…about molepeople.

Bev licked her lips. "That doesn't seem like a coincidence, Biscuit. Grant had been telling me about Eldred's rants. Nog overheard him. And you know, the other door to Pigsend isn't far from here. The one Shamus creates." She looked down at the laelaps. "He was able to turn horses into caterpillars and weapons into bread… Do you think he's capable of cursing people?" She bit her lip. "And if so, what quarrel did he have with the others?"

Biscuit, predictably, didn't answer.

"Can you tell if the door to Lower Pigsend is still open?" Bev asked.

The laelaps wagged his tail.

"Take me to it."

She followed Biscuit out of Eldred's house, down the road, and off his fields. As she crested a large hill on the edge of Eldred's lands, she spotted Shamus. He stood in front of a tunnel on the opposite hillside, staring at his timepiece and tapping his foot. Nog wasn't anywhere to be seen—an indictment or an alibi?

Bev marched down the hillside, causing Shamus to jump in shock and brandish his wand. When he saw Bev, he relaxed, though he kept his weapon at the ready.

"What do you want?" he snapped. "Don't you usually go through Merv's house to get to Lower Pigsend?"

"Is Nog back yet?" Bev asked.

"Not yet. But I assume he's probably still running errands. Lots for him to do, you know," Shamus said with a scowl. "Why?"

"I'm sure Percival told you about the folks in a magical coma," Bev said. "I—"

"He has," Shamus said. "Magical potion-enhanced curse. He also told you the ingredients were sourced out of Middleburg, so I fail to see why you're telling *me* about it."

"Because I saw Officer Nog at the farmers' market," she said. "He overheard Grant Klose telling me about Eldred Nest, who lives over that hill, ranting and raving about molepeople in Pigsend."

"Merv," Shamus said. "Still not—"

"I think he meant you and Nog," Bev cut him off. "Because, as I said, he lives right over that hill. It's not a stretch to think he's seen you standing here. It doesn't look like you've taken any precautions…"

Shamus bristled. "I take *plenty* of precautions."

"Then how come I snuck up on you?" Bev asked with a knowing smile.

"Maybe I should move the tunnel," he muttered. "Or use Merv's, but goodness, that moleman is *such* a—"

"*More importantly*," Bev said, "I found Eldred in the same magical coma as everyone else. Hence my question about Nog's whereabouts."

"So you think Nog's the one cursing people?" Shamus scoffed. "He doesn't have that kind of magic."

"He did during the solstice," Bev said. "And the person casting the curse needs a magical boost from a potion. Nog fits that description."

Shamus clicked his tongue. "I suppose you're right. But a potion to enhance magic is quite complex, and requires a keen eye. Nog doesn't have those skills. So where would he get it?"

"Gerry?" Bev asked.

"*That's* not likely," Shamus said. "Gerry can barely handle willow root tinctures and cleaning potions. He doesn't have the ability to create something like that. Not to mention, *as we've established*, the ingredients came from Middleburg. How would Gerry get them to make the potion?" He gestured to the tunnel. "Nothing gets past here without my knowledge. And I doubt your moleman friend would entertain Gerry without telling you."

Bev crossed her arms. He was making too much sense. "Could *you* take a potion and curse people?"

"I don't need a potion to curse people," Shamus said with a glare. "And frankly, I'm offended that you think I have so little magic it'd be necessary.

Just because Percival is older and more skilled doesn't mean I couldn't curse someone outright." He tightened his hold on his wand. "Do you want to test that theory? I'd be happy to show you."

"I'm fine, thanks," Bev said, inching backward. "And I apologize. I didn't mean to cause offense."

Just at that moment, Nog came strolling up the drive with the wagon full of fruits, vegetables, and grains. His potion was wearing off, and his skin was taking on a distinct green color.

He scowled when he spotted Bev. "What are you doing here?"

"Bev thinks you're cursing people," Shamus said. "Is that true?"

"Cursing people?" He snorted. "How could I have the ability to do that?"

"You had a lot of ability during the solstice," Bev said.

Nog grunted, but Shamus brandished his wand again. "There's an easy way to find out. Nog, show me your hands."

The goblin let out a grunt of annoyance but did as he was asked. Shamus tapped his wand against Nog's fingers, and nothing happened.

"There, you happy?" Nog snapped.

"No," Bev said with a sigh. "Because I don't have any other leads. Nothing connects any of the victims, other than they're all customers of our local apothecary, which makes me feel like someone's trying to frame him. But for what purpose? Bernard doesn't have any enemies other than Gerry, especially enemies with the ability to curse people."

Shamus actually looked sorry for her. "You know," he said softly, "Winston serves a lot of people. Including more than a few in Pigsend, as I understand it. If you're looking for the person who made the potion, I might ask him who else is on his client list. Might come up with some new ideas."

"Do you think he'd tell me?" Bev asked.

He shrugged, turning to follow Nog into the tunnel. "Can't hurt to ask."

When Bev got back to the inn, Howser was in the front room, and shook his head when Bev told him the next victim. She declined to mention that he had a vial in his hand, as that didn't seem relevant. It didn't fit the pattern, and they were looking for a curse-caster, not a potion-maker.

"Eldred is Trent's neighbor," Howser said thoughtfully. "Do you think maybe that's related?"

"It all seems so random," Bev said. "Which is unnerving. Because the more victims fall, the more I feel like someone is picking off people at their leisure." She shook herself. "*Someone* has to have seen something."

"Maybe we'll get some answers at the town meeting tonight," Howser said.

"Goodness, I nearly forgot all about that," Bev

said, glancing at the clock. It would be tight, but she could get everything done in time. "I'm expected to make a crisp. Cranberry apple."

"Why?"

"It'll be baked with iron," Bev said. "Might help deflect some of the curse, but I have my doubts. I think Hendry wants to show people she's doing something to stop it. I'm sure I'll be called up to speak, as usual. But I don't have anything to say."

Howser swallowed. "You aren't going to…erm, mention my wife, are you?"

Bev shook her head. "Sherr—Penny's reasons for staying hidden are good ones. And now that Max and Eldred have been attacked, too… I don't see why she'd want to hurt them. Unless there were two more sides to their love polygon."

Howser chuckled. "No, I don't believe so. But since we have no suspects and no motive, maybe we look at this from a higher level."

"What do you mean?"

"Well, if the attacks *are* random, and there's no evidence, maybe someone is trying to send a message. Convey some idea." He tilted his head. "Exactly what message and to whom, I haven't a clue. But they've got a goal in mind. And I don't think they're going to stop until that goal is achieved."

Bev mulled over his idea as she returned downstairs. Dinner was steaming and bubbling away, and her rosemary bread loaves were cooling, but she had that darned crisp to make.

The apples were waiting next to the cranberries, so Bev started by chopping them and adding them to one of three baking pans. She couldn't be sure who'd be in attendance tonight, but the most well-attended town meetings numbered about fifty. As she chopped and tossed the pieces into the pans, she let her mind wander.

Although Howser seemed to think the attacks were random, Bev wasn't ready to give up on the connection theory. After all, it couldn't have been a coincidence that Eldred had been attacked so soon after Nog had been informed of his ranting. Although the goblin's hands had been clean of magic, *something* told her Eldred's attack wasn't random. Nog and Gerry had *somewhat* worked together in the past, and Nog had shown the ability to cast magic during the solstice. But why would Nog want to attack Trent, Herman, Etheldra, and Max, too?

She kept ruminating over the same questions as she added a few palmfuls of cinnamon to the apples, relying on their natural sweetness to come out when it baked. Once that was mixed, she stirred in the whole cranberries, dotting the plump red berries in with the white flesh of the apples. And to that, Bev added her satchels of nails. It had been plenty for the solstice hijinks, and though Bev still had her doubts about its efficacy, at least it was something.

In another bowl, she combined butter and sugar from the bakers, oats from her root cellar, and more cinnamon until it came together. She sprinkled the topping evenly over the three pans then slid them into the oven to bake. Within minutes, the entire kitchen smelled absolutely divine. Protective or not, at least the people of Pigsend would have a delicious treat.

As she worked, she replayed her conversation with Gerry in Lower Pigsend. How he'd offered to help *only* if Bev would put in a good word for him. She could see a world in which he'd created a cursed potion for Nog to use to attack his brother's customers, framing his brother, so he could then come to the rescue. Shamus had said nothing got past him, but *what if* Nog had gotten the ingredients from Winston secretly, and smuggled them into Pigsend to Gerry? The apothecary made the potion, Nog then cursed—

Shamus cast a spell on him, Bev reminded herself. *Nog hadn't used magic.*

She sighed as she looked at the ceiling. "This is such a mess, Biscuit."

He let out a low ruff.

"You're right. We do have one more person to question," Bev said. "Winston will be in town this evening. Can you keep an eye on Bernard and let me know when he leaves his shop?"

Biscuit wagged his tail but didn't move.

"Oh, right." Bev chopped up half an apple and gave it to him. "Here you go. I'll save you some dinner, too."

Satisfied, the laelaps trotted out the kitchen door.

~

The town meeting would get underway around seven, so at six, Bev served dinner. She'd expected a few more faces, even with Max and Etheldra upstairs, but only Bardoff came to eat. He, like everyone else, seemed jumpy, as if something was going to pop out of the woodwork and curse him, too.

"Well, I had half a mind not to come tonight," he said, poking at the bread. "I mean, Max and Etheldra eat here. What if that's what they're targeting?"

"Trent and Herman don't, though, and neither does Eldred," Bev said gently.

"Suppose you're right." He shuddered. "I've heard you've been looking into it. Where the heck has Rustin been?"

Bev honestly didn't know. Hendry had said he didn't want to attract the attention of his superiors by going to Middleburg, but to her knowledge, he hadn't even gone to any of the victims' houses. Then again, she didn't keep track of him, so perhaps he had, and like her, hadn't found anything worth sharing.

"I'm sure he'll tell us everything he's discovered at the town meeting," Bev said, after a moment. "He's probably been researching or…"

Bardoff gave her a sideways look.

"Erm. Well." Bev cleared her throat. "He's the sheriff. He told me he's got to prove himself in order to keep his job. So here's hoping."

"It feels like we're all vulnerable," he said. "I only had two kids show up for class today. Everyone's scared. No one knows who'll be next." He made a face. "The only thing keeping me sane is it that appears to be people in the older crowd. I'm not young by any measure, but I don't seem to be in the targeted demographic."

"That's true," Bev said.

"And you haven't a clue what connects them?" Bardoff asked. "Not that it's your job to figure these things out, but…"

"You know," Bev faked a smile, "these town meetings have a way of bringing out all kinds of opinions and ideas. I'm sure someone's seen something I've missed. I'm confident something will shake loose soon."

"I hear we're supposed to bring a bowl and spoon to the town meeting," Bardoff said. "Did I mishear that, or…?"

"Hendry asked me to make…" She considered her words. "A little something. An apple-cranberry crisp. For morale."

"Just morale?"

"I might've added something for protection, too," Bev said. "A little infusion of iron."

His eyes brightened. "Do you think it'll work?"

As much as she wanted to calm his nerves, Bev couldn't lie to the schoolteacher. "Honestly, Bardoff, I don't know. It might help, but a curse is a powerful bit of magic, you know? A little iron in the system might not be any match for it."

He sighed, deflating. "You know, I thought we were supposed to be done with all this magical nonsense. Isn't that why the queen outlawed it? Everyone who was supposed to be a danger to the community should've been taken care of, right?"

Bev didn't have an answer for him. "Whoever's doing this has an agenda. I can't figure out what that agenda is."

"Seems to me someone's having a bit of fun keeping us all awake at night," Bardoff said. "Perhaps they should go ahead and put me in a trance like the others. I haven't gotten a wink of sleep in days."

Bev nodded to the clean bowls and utensils. "If you'd like to borrow a bowl and spoon to take with you to the town meeting, you can."

"I'm not attending," Bardoff said, rising. "It's the perfect place for whoever's causing trouble to cause more trouble. I'm going to go home and lock my doors. And hope that whoever's terrorizing this town decides to move on soon."

Chapter Eighteen

As Bev still had most of an entire dinner already made, she decided to take a leaf out of Hendry's book and bring it to the town meeting. She dipped across the street to ask Vellora and Ida if they wanted dinner and to help carry, and of course, they were happy to assist—after helping themselves to a plate.

"That was perfect, thank you, Bev," Ida said, happily tapping her stomach, before glancing up. "Poor Max. And Eldred! How random is that? Who'd have any cause to bother Eldred Nest?"

"The molepeople," Vellora said with a half-smile.

Bev forced her face to remain neutral. "I hope someone's got something to share. Maybe they saw something. Or heard something."

"Howser's coming, right?" Ida asked.

Bev nodded. "But I don't think he'll have much to share, either. The patients are in good health in every other way other than they're asleep."

"How's Earl doing?" Vellora asked.

"Hanging in there," Bev said. "I brought him a plate earlier. He's not going to the town meeting, either. Says he doesn't want to leave in case Etheldra wakes up."

The butchers shared a look that was a mix of adoration and pity. "I hope you know I wouldn't leave your side if you were caught in a magical coma," Ida said to Vellora.

The other butcher cooed back, "How romantic."

Bev smiled.

With the Witzels' help, Bev carried the three pans of crisp to the town hall. Ida snuck a piece of apple and topping then made a face and almost spat it out.

"Yep, can definitely taste the iron," she said. "I wish you'd made some without. It looks heavenly."

"If it keeps you safe, you'd better eat all of it," Vellora countered. "I'm still not convinced this isn't related to the Harvest Festival. And you and Bev would be prime targets."

"Wouldn't they have targeted us already?" Bev asked. "Especially since we're trying to figure out who's behind it? You know, get us out of the way?"

"Good point," Ida said with a nod. "What do you think it means that they haven't?"

Bev still wasn't sure about the Nog-Gerry-Winston connection, and until she spoke to the merchant, she didn't want to cast stones. Especially as there was a chance Bernard wasn't the only person in town getting magical ingredients from the merchant. Maybe Bathilda, who lived next to Herman, had a hidden agenda against all the other farmers. It was far-fetched, but Bev could go visit her if she didn't—

"Bev?" Ida prompted her. "What do you think it means?"

"I don't know," she said, after a long pause. "But I have a feeling there's some other angle we haven't seen yet."

They arrived at the town hall, which was only half full even so close to the start time. Hendry greeted them eagerly and beckoned Bev and the others to place the crisp on the table behind her. Everyone seated had a bowl and spoon in hand, and more than a few people eyed the leftover dinner pans hungrily.

"I think you made too much," Hendry said. "Looks like this is going to be our crowd tonight. Did you make all of this with iron?"

"Erm, no. Not the meat, in any case—"

"Don't be silly, of course you did," Hendry said with a wink. "Because I don't think *that* pan of crisp is going to feed this crowd, even as small as it is."

Bev frowned, taking stock of those in attendance. At a normal town meeting, it would be packed full, with people standing around the edges and others crammed in on the benches. But now, there was ample space for everyone, and the ones milling around seemed to want to socialize.

"Shouldn't we give people a bit more time to show up?" Bev asked.

"It's seven," Hendry said simply, walking to the front of the room and clapping her hands. "Thank you so much for coming out. I understand everyone is nervous about the current—"

"Attacks?" Rosie Kelooke sat in the front row, her arms folded across her chest.

"Incidents," Hendry said with a tight smile. "We're all a bit on edge, but I want to say up front that we are working on it. Bernard's been burning the candle at both ends trying different things. And Doc Howser assures me that, while the victims are unconscious, they're perfectly healthy. As soon as we figure out exactly what has befallen them, they'll wake up and be right as rain."

Rosie let out a *harrumph* and crossed her ankles.

"What are you doing about these *incidents*?" Shasta asked, sitting on the other side of the room.

"More specifically, do we know why Etheldra and the others were targeted?" Stella asked.

Hendry glanced at Bev, who shook her head.

Hendry smiled. "Why don't we let Bev tell us all about it?"

Bev grumbled but rose and walked to the front of the room. A sea of worried faces stared back at her. Bev couldn't remember a time when everyone had looked so unnerved.

"Erm, well." Bev cleared her throat. "We're working on theories."

"Such as?" Hendry prompted. "Why don't you start at the beginning, Bev? Fill everyone in on what we've been up to. I'm sure they've heard a variation of it. Might as well tell them everything."

Bev told them about finding Trent, and how there wasn't any sign of magic on or around him. Then, about Herman sneaking around his house, and how, not even a few hours later, she'd found *him* in the same state. She skipped over the parts about Lower Pigsend, jumping straight to how they'd thought perhaps it was an attempt to discredit the Harvest Festival.

"But now that Max and Eldred have been attacked, too, that seems less likely," Bev said.

"Well, what *do* you know?" Apolinary McGraw, the local seamstress, called from the front row. Beside her, Pip and Holly Norris, the farriers, gripped each other's hands and bit their lips. "Because it seems like you don't have any idea what's going on."

"Honestly, we don't," Bev said, earning a gasp of

worry from the crowd.

"What Bev *means* is that we have working theories, and we've taken steps to ensure everyone is protected," Hendry butted in with a dirty look. "To wit, Bev has brought a spread of food and delicious apple cranberry crisp, all with an iron infusion. Everyone, take a bit. It will help protect you against the curse or whatever it is floating around town. Come, come. Line up and get it. It smells divine. Bev, do the honors and serve everyone, will you?"

Hendry deftly changed the tone of the room, and before long, there was a queue to get a bite. As she scooped, people murmured to each other about leaving town and canceling the Harvest Festival.

"We are *not* canceling the Harvest Festival," Ida said, loud enough for the crowd to hear. "We will figure this out soon. I promise."

"You have five victims," Rosie said. "Five victims, and no leads. There doesn't even seem to be a connection between them."

"Other than that they're all old," Shasta said. "Maybe someone's trying to eradicate all the old biddies in town."

Rosie covered her mouth in horror.

"I don't think that's what's going on," Bev said. Her gaze went to the clock—Bernard, who was absent from the town meeting, would be meeting with Winston any minute now. Bev needed to find a good excuse to leave, one that wouldn't make the crowd more worried than they already were.

"What else can we do to protect ourselves?" Pip asked.

"The food should do the trick," Hendry said. "And I'm sure the culprit will reveal himself soon, right, Bev?"

Bev was starting to get the feeling Hendry was setting her up, especially if the food—most of which *wasn't* baked with iron and willow—didn't work to stave off evil magic. Bev could imagine a mob of angry townsfolk at her door, demanding to know why she'd only given them an illusion of safety. But the tension in the room faded as the people ate, and even Rosie seemed less grumpy. Perhaps even an illusion would help them sleep better tonight. Of course, that wouldn't work if their attacker decided to go for someone else.

A small golden object appeared at the door. Biscuit.

"Erm, I need to check something at the inn," Bev said to Hendry. "Do you mind if I—"

"Not at *all*," Hendry said with a knowing smile. "Are there any more questions?" Hendry asked. "If not, everyone head back home. Lock your doors and all that, but don't fret. We are working diligently to solve this problem. I hope to provide everyone with a positive update tomorrow!"

Even with every eye on her, Bev was able to slip

out quickly through the side door, and before long, she was walking along the dirt path, following the white tip of Biscuit's tail in the moonlight. She hadn't a clue where Bernard would be meeting Winston, but as Biscuit turned north, the answer became obvious. The dark forest—a patch of magical, sentient trees—was the site of many secret magical transactions. Bev had seen wyvern eggs being sold and barus baubles being handed off. It made sense Winston also did many of his transactions here.

She slowed as she approached. What kind of mood would the forest be in tonight? The last few times, it had let her pass without a problem. Tonight, it seemed to be in a similar humor, moving brambles and thorns and branches aside for her and Biscuit.

"Glad we've come to an understanding," Bev muttered.

Voices echoed ahead, and as the clearing came into view, she spotted Winston with Bernard. The merchant wore his trademark emotionless expression as he watched Bernard poke through the bag but the apothecary was looking more exhausted and harried than he had before. It was hard for Bev to believe *this* man was responsible in any capacity.

"Well?" Winston prompted.

"It'll be fine," Bernard said. "A bit old, but—"

"Beggars can't be choosers in this day and age,"

Winston said, holding out his hand. "The queen's people are squeezing my suppliers, but we get by."

Bernard handed him a bag then left without another word—luckily in the opposite direction that Bev had come. Winston counted the coins for a moment then lazily pocketed the money and turned to go.

Bev rose from her hiding spot. "Winston?"

The merchant stopped, straightening before spinning to her. Bev hadn't really had more than a single conversation with him, though she'd overheard two now. She approached with a little trepidation, keeping her distance and grateful that Biscuit stood in front of her.

Winston surveyed her with a curious expression that settled into a smile. "What can I do for you, Bev?"

She blinked. "You know who I am?"

"You're quite famous," he said with a nod. "What can I help you with?"

"I wanted to talk about the cursed people in town," Bev said. "Have you heard about them?"

"I've heard a few things."

"Did you hear they've been cursed by someone who took a potion first?" Bev asked. "And that potion was made with ingredients from Middleburg?"

He stared at her blankly. "Fascinating."

Bev clicked her tongue. "Are you the one

supplying those ingredients for the potion the curse-caster is taking? If so, you have to tell me—"

"I supply a lot of ingredients to a lot of people." He lifted a shoulder. "And part of my very lucrative business model is not sharing who my clients are, nor what they do with what I bring them." He smiled. "To anyone. Including nosy innkeepers."

"I'm trying to figure out what's going on," Bev said. "These people are innocent, and without knowing what's wrong with them, we can't wake them up." She gestured toward Pigsend to the south. "Please. The townsfolk are scared out of their minds. If you could give me some kind of... Well, some hint so I'm not still fumbling around in the dark."

He sniffed.

"Please?" Bev reached into her pocket and pulled out a gold coin.

He held out his hand and she tossed it to him. "I'll answer one question. But not about what I sell or to whom."

Bev thought for a moment, looking back at the spot Bernard had vacated. There were a hundred questions she could ask, but most of them were the straightforward kind that he certainly wouldn't answer. But she did have one question that met his criteria.

"Have you told Bernard his brother's in Lower Pigsend?" Bev asked. "Or anything about Lower Pigsend at all?"

"I haven't told him about Lower Pigsend," he said. "And I don't know anything about his brother."

"Gerry, the, erm, feathered apothecary in Lower Pigsend," Bev said. "That's Bernard's brother. Have you met him?"

"Not…in person," Winston said. "But I've used his services in the past. Through an intermediary."

"Used his services… So people buy tinctures from Gerry?" Bev asked, quickly connecting the dots. Gerry would have access to more magical ingredients than Bernard would. "And you deliver them?"

"People are in need of potions for all manner of things," he said. "Sometimes they want the ingredients. Sometimes the potions. I *obviously* help where possible. But sometimes even combining the ingredients up here is too dangerous. So they have to be made in a safer place."

Bev nodded slowly. "So…that's how the people in Lower Pigsend were able to pay for all the goods you smuggled in for them. People wanted magic, you got it bottled from Gerry, and you paid Gerry handsomely for the effort."

"I can neither confirm nor deny that sort of transaction took place or who got paid for what."

No wonder Gerry was still so busy; the majority of his clients were outside of Lower Pigsend. And no wonder Percival had wanted him to stick around, even as unskilled as he was. If there were no other apothecaries in Lower Pigsend, they could no longer create the potions that were funding their existence.

"Have you brought a potion from Gerry to—"

"As I said, I don't tell people about my other clients," he replied. "Now, if that's all, I've got to get going. I hear Karolina Hunter's around, and she would be absolutely *overjoyed* to make my acquaintance."

"She's in Middleburg," Bev said. "Or she was the other day."

"Mm. Well." He gave her a small bow. "If you'll excuse me."

"One more question." Bev pulled out another coin.

"You'd better make it a good one," he said, taking it from her. "As you've already taken up more of my time than I'd like."

"Have you ever given Bernard an incorrect ingredient?" Bev asked. "Maybe he asked for one thing, and you gave him another? Maybe because someone wanted you to?"

He snorted. "You must have a low opinion of Bernard."

"Why?"

"Any apothecary worth his salt knows exactly what he's putting into his potion vials," he said. "They should be able to look at, smell, touch, perhaps even taste the ingredient and know what it is—even without a label. Why do you think they spent so many years in school? They've got to have an encyclopedic knowledge of every plant and potion out there."

"O-oh." Bev deflated. "So you couldn't have pulled one over on Bernard?"

"Not Bernard, no." He shook his head. "A lesser apothecary? Probably. But Bernard? No way." He adjusted his shirt. "Now, if you'll excuse me…"

Bev let him go. That the wily merchant wouldn't share anything more than he wanted Bev to know. Still, she'd gotten a *bit* more insight. Gerry, for all his faults, was perhaps the only one in Lower Pigsend actually making something that could be sold in the wider world. Did that have any bearing on this current situation, or was it just an interesting fact?

The journey back to Pigsend was long, but only because Bev didn't know what else to do. Her theories about Nog being the culprit were fading, as was the idea of Gerry being involved somehow. With no other suspects, she came back to what Doc Howser had said on their way back from Eldred's house.

"Someone is trying to send a message," Bev muttered as the inn came into view. "But what message are they trying to send? And to whom?"

As she opened the door, her breath caught in her throat. Karolina Hunter stood at the front desk, a disgusted look on her face.

"Goodness, where in the world have you been?" she said. "I require a room. And to see all the victims of this curse."

Chapter Nineteen

It took Bev a moment to realize what she'd said. "You're staying here?"

"Yes. I've been told the victims are all at the inn," she drawled. "Unless there's some pressing reason you *don't* want me to see them."

"Nope." Bev couldn't believe her next words. "Maybe you can help us figure out what's going on."

Karolina snorted. "I can certainly try."

Bev found a room for her and gave her the key, but the soldier was more interested in the victims. Bev let her into the room where Eldred, Max, Herman, and Trent were sleeping.

"I thought there were five?" she asked.

"Etheldra's in the next room over," Bev said.

"Earl, her husband, wanted to stay with her."

"I see." Karolina bent down next to Trent, poking his cheek. "And how long have they been like this?"

"A few days now," Bev said. "Trent, that one, was the first to go down. Then Herman, then Etheldra. Max this morning. Eldred was this afternoon." She cleared her throat. "What do you reckon?"

"I reckon this town is once again a hotbed for magical nonsense," Karolina said, rising. "We should've put that river stopper in permanently."

And caused the destruction of the whole town. "It's clear someone's targeting them intentionally. But I can't figure out what the motive or goal is."

"What does that sorry excuse for a sheriff think?" Karolina asked.

"Rustin?" Bev hadn't even seen him at the town meeting. Where was he?

Exactly as she had that thought, Rustin came barreling through the front door. He huffed and puffed before he straightened, smiling at Karolina and brushing back his hair as if nothing were amiss.

"I heard you were in town," he said. "Welcome back to Pigsend—"

"I was monitoring the town meeting." Bev hadn't seen her, but maybe she'd arrived after Bev had left to speak with Winston. "You weren't there. Where were you?"

"Erm, at home," he said, rubbing the back of his head. "I didn't have anything to add—

"You're the sheriff," Karolina snapped. "You should've been front and center."

He glanced at Bev, perhaps hoping she would save him. When she didn't, his cheeks reddened. "I, erm, was looking into things. Of course. Thinking about all we've learned. Trying to look for, erm, something else. Yes, that's it."

Bev rolled her eyes. If Rustin was trying to inspire confidence, he surely wasn't succeeding.

"So to what do we owe the pleasure of your visit?" Rustin said, his voice growing higher.

Karolina stared at him as if he had two heads. "Why do you think I'm here, Rustin? You've got a magical menace on the loose, and you've done nothing to stop it."

"Oh, I have, too!" Rustin said with a gasp. "I've been working with Bev."

That was a lie, but Bev held her tongue, because it didn't seem to matter to Karolina.

"*Bev* is a civilian," Karolina said. "You, on the other hand, are the queen's representative. You should be the one leading the case." She crossed her arms over her chest. "Do you even know how many victims there are?"

Rustin opened and closed his mouth. Bev held up five fingers behind Karolina's back. "Five!" he exclaimed.

"Right." Karolina glared at Bev; a warning to stay out of it. "I want to know everything you know about what's going on."

He cleared his throat. "Erm, well, I know there are five victims. They're all asleep. We don't know why." He smiled. "And that's all we know."

"That's pretty pathetic," Karolina said.

"Actually, he's spot on, there," Bev said. "We've had lots of theories, but we can't figure out a pattern. Especially the last couple of victims, they seem disconnected from the others. Eldred, specifically. I doubt he's ever had a conversation with Max in his life."

Karolina rubbed her chin. "They're all old, though."

"They are old," Bev agreed. "But there are lots of older folks in Pigsend. Why haven't they been attacked? Why these specific people?"

"Sounds to me like it's random," Karolina said.

"Yes, but for what purpose?" Bev said. "Other than scaring the town half to death."

"What about the Harvest Festival?" Rustin said, sounding like he was trying to be helpful. "Didn't you guys think that was the reason?" At Karolina's scrutinizing glare, he wilted. "I mean, didn't *we* think that was the reason? Don't we think that's the reason?" He nodded, as if content that he'd salvaged his mistake. "Right, Bev?"

"We could go back to that," Bev said. "It's

possible someone from Middleburg is eager to move the festival. Miranda Twinsly is certainly trying to use the chaos to her benefit."

"It's no one in Middleburg," Karolina said. "And I'm here precisely so the Harvest Festival can be held in a few weeks."

"You *want* to hold the Harvest Festival here?" Bev found that very strange. "Why?"

"That's my business," she snapped. "You're the one who found them all?"

"All except Etheldra," Bev said.

"And no one thought that was suspicious?" Karolina said, looking at Rustin, clearly talking to him.

"I'm not cursing people," Bev said with a thin smile. "I always get roped into solving these things. Trent, I was at his house to get paperwork. I found Herman when I went to speak with him about who might be out to get him. Earl was the one who found Etheldra."

"And the other two?"

"Max and I were discussing the case, and he went to the backroom to get something for me," Bev said. "Eldred, I found at his house."

"Maybe the person who's cursing people is keen on sending *you* a message, Bev," Rustin said with a bright grin.

Bev blinked at him. "What message is that, Rustin?"

He opened and closed his mouth.

Karolina kept staring at her, to the point where Bev let out a breath of annoyance. "I'm not the one cursing people. I've got an inn to run, a Harvest Festival to compete in, and bread to bake. If anything, I'm glad you're here because I'd like to wash my hands of all this and let someone else run around looking for answers."

Karolina snorted. "Unfortunately, you're already *involved*, so you're going to have to stay involved. Tomorrow, we're going to scour every single inch of this town until we figure out who's behind it." She turned to Rustin. "And I want you here at seven. Understand?"

Rustin saluted.

"I *will* get to the bottom of this," Karolina said. "And someone's going away in handcuffs tomorrow, guilty or not."

~

Although Bev liked Rustin personally, she couldn't help but agree with Karolina about his job performance. It was fine when the town was quiet, or when the culprit was an innocent kid or a drunk goblin. But putting people in magical comas seemed a step too far, even for Bev's capacity for forgiveness.

Still, Karolina's presence meant precautions needed to be made for the innocent magical folks, especially those across the street. In the morning, before the bakers arrived with the morning pastries,

Bev let them know Karolina was next door. Allen was less concerned than Lillie, but they both thought it was a good idea to keep a low profile until the soldier left town.

"Not that I think she's here to look for magical bakers," Bev said. "But if nothing else comes up, she might want to make sure the trip was worth her while."

Lillie nodded. "That town meeting seemed like a bust. Though I could tell you added iron to that crumble last night."

Allen made a face. "Yeah, it was quite acrid."

"I'll be sure to make another one soon without it," Bev said.

When Bev got back to the inn, Karolina was downstairs talking with Doc Howser. The doctor seemed uncomfortable with her questions but answered them calmly.

"In my experience, it looks to be a magical coma," he said.

"And you have a lot of experience with magical ailments?" Karolina asked.

He gave her a tight smile. "I've had a long career."

She sniffed, as if that were an arrestable offense.

"Erm, I brought muffins," Bev announced, holding the basket aloft. "How are our patients doing?"

"The same as yesterday," Howser replied. "As I

was explaining to Ms. Hunter here, Bernard and I have been working around the clock doing tests and searching for answers."

"I'd like to speak with Mr. Rickshaw," she said. "And hear what sort of *testing* he's been doing."

Howser's eyes narrowed, but he nodded. "I'll be sure to tell him to swing by the inn."

"No need." Karolina looked at Bev. "Rustin should be here any minute now if he wants to keep his job."

Howser excused himself, saying he needed to get upstairs to check on the patients again, leaving Bev and Karolina alone.

Karolina snatched up one of the muffins and sniffed it. "I see the baker next door has hired an assistant."

Bev nodded, keeping her face neutral. "They've been quite busy. Allen almost got married—long story—but his cake was so well received that everyone in the area is clamoring for their goods, and—"

"What's her story?" Karolina said. "The assistant?"

"Lillie?" Bev shrugged and used her rehearsed line. "Not sure. She came to the inn a few months ago. Seemed to be looking for a new place to put down roots. She and Allen got along well, and she decided to stick around."

"I see." Karolina surveyed the inn. "Seems

everything got put right since the last time I was here."

"Erm, yes." Bev wasn't going to mention the sinkholes. "You know, we've had a slate of soldiers coming through town. Did you know Allen is Zed Mackey's son?"

"Zed Mackey? Commander Zed Mackey?" That actually surprised her. "No wonder he was so keen to come back."

"Yes, well, they weren't on the best of terms, but they're all right now," Bev said. "He and Dag Flanigan seem to have circled back a few times. Must be the delicious rosemary bread."

Karolina stared at her. "You think?"

"That's my thought," Bev said.

"Where in the world is that useless sheriff?" Karolina muttered. It was a few minutes to seven, and Bev rather hoped Rustin would be early, if only to raise his standing with his superior officer a little. But it was two minutes after when he came in, rubbing his eyes and yawning.

"Morning, all," he said. "I—Oh, are those muffins?" His face lit up as he walked over to get one.

Before he could, Karolina snatched them away. "You're late. Let's go."

Karolina wanted to visit each attack site, starting with Trent's house. The home was unlocked—and untouched—since Bev had found Herman here. Karolina swept the room, her eagle eyes roving over every single inch of the house. Of course, she found nothing more than Bev had when she'd first looked through the place.

"And you said you saw the second victim in here?" Karolina asked.

"Yes, erm, he had a locket on him," Bev said. "But I think he was taking advantage of his nemesis being incapacitated."

"Where's the locket now?" Karolina asked.

"I put it back on Trent," Bev said. "Since it was his to begin with."

To answer Karolina's questioning stare, Bev told her about the long-ago love triangle with Etheldra's sister. "But I don't think that's related. Not with Max and Eldred being attacked as well."

"Right." Karolina poked her head out the door. "Rustin? Find anything?"

Rustin, who was sitting on the front porch, jumped up. "Erm, nope. Not yet. Nothing out here. Everything's on the up and up."

Karolina sniffed. "Who was next?"

Herman was next, but Bev suggested they go down the road to Eldred's house, as it was closer. Karolina agreed, and once again, scoured the house, finding nothing. This time, Rustin joined them inside the house, but he was about as useless.

"I found him here," Bev said, pointing to the

chair. "He'd taken a vial of something."

"A vial?" She frowned. "That's important, don't you think?"

"None of the other victims had one," Bev said.

Karolina stared at the floor, thinking about something. "What's the story about this apothecary?"

"Bernard?" Bev said slowly. "He's been trying to find a cure."

"Has he now?" She turned on her heel. "I wonder if he might know a bit more than he's letting on. He and that doctor seem to know more about magic than they should."

"And thank goodness they do," Bev said. "Because otherwise, we'd really be up a creek. Imagine not knowing what a magical coma is. The town would've been in an uproar because they thought people were dropping like flies. We might've even buried Trent or Herman had we not known they were asleep." She shook her head. "Goodness, the thought of it."

Bev's hypotheticals didn't seem to sway Karolina. "Come. Let's go have a chat with him."

"I thought you told Howser—"

"I want to speak with him at his shop. Something tells me I'll find something of interest there."

Bev hoped Howser had given Bernard a heads

up about the soldier, and that all the ingredients he'd gotten from Winston would be hidden. But as they drew closer to the apothecary shop, Bev's dread grew. Karolina had said she was going to arrest someone, and it wasn't a stretch to think she might take the apothecary, guilty or not.

The door swung open, and Stella looked up, swallowing hard. "Erm. Bev. Hi. Who's this?"

"This is Ms. Hunter," Bev said. "She's a member of the queen's service. Is Bernard back there?"

Stella nodded, holding her hands as she stepped away from the counter. Karolina didn't wait for directions, walking right into the back room.

"There's magic in here," Karolina said almost immediately.

Bev's heart sank. "What do you mean? How can you tell?"

"Can't *you* tell?" Karolina replied, but her focus was on Rustin, who'd slowly sauntered in, gazing around as if he'd never been back here before. "Rustin?"

"Erm, what?" He snapped his attention to her. "Something about magic? You think there's some here? I certainly can't tell."

Karolina scoffed and marched to the table where Bernard did his experiments. She scanned the contents—vials and open bags and droppers and scribbled notes—then, with a knowing smile, she lifted a small bag from the center of the table. The one Winston had given to Bernard the night before.

"Found it," Karolina said.

"Really?" Rustin eyed it closely. "You think?"

"I don't think…" Bev started then measured her words. "I thought we were looking for someone who cast a curse? What kind of magic's in that bag?"

"It doesn't matter," Karolina said. "It's magic. Magic is illegal. That's good enough for me."

Rustin took the bag from her, sniffing it. "You think this is magic? I'm not sure. It smells normal to me. What's magical about it?"

Karolina clicked her tongue loudly. "Are you telling me you don't even know how to find magic when it's right in front of your nose? What good are you to anyone, then?"

"Oh, um. I do…" Rustin cleared his throat. "I do a lot to protect the peace, and—"

"And you can't even do the bare minimum." She snatched the bag back from him. "How long has your apothecary been dealing with magic under your nose, hm? Is anyone else magical in this town? I heard there were all manner of things happening during the solstice. Lucky Zed Mackey was here to keep a handle on it, but what if he wasn't? Would you have let all that magical nonsense go unchecked?"

"I—"

"I've been here *one day,* and I already found the culprit," Karolina said.

"But you haven't," Bev interrupted. "I—"

"That's enough out of you, innkeeper," Karolina said. "You said you wanted to wash your hands of this, so wash your hands of it." She turned back to Rustin. "I don't know if you knew the apothecary was dealing under the table with magic and looked the other way, or if you're so bad, you didn't think to check him—"

"I swear, I had no idea Bernard was using magic," Rustin said.

Bev winced. That was *not* the right thing to say.

Karolina let out a weary sigh. "I'm going to go find the apothecary. Rustin, you're fired."

Chapter Twenty

Rustin stared at her, blinking as if he hadn't heard her. "What?"

"You're fired," Karolina said, holding out her hand. "Give me your badge and go home. You're no longer needed in this investigation. Or this town."

"You can't just… I have superiors in…"

"Your superiors asked me to evaluate you for job fitness," she said. "And I'm not sorry to say I've found it lacking. There's clearly a spate of magical mischief happening in this town, all under your nose. And that you've failed not only to stop any of it but even *notice* it is a dereliction of duty that cannot be ignored." She lifted her chin. "Now as I said, hand over your badge. You are no longer a member of Her Majesty's service."

Rustin unclipped his badge from his tunic and handed it over, his face still a mask of shock.

Bev held her tongue. Nothing Karolina said was untrue, although Bev had a suspicion Hendry wanted it that way. It was easier to hide the innocent magical creatures from Her Majesty when the man assigned to keep the peace was a bit thickheaded. Still, it hurt Bev's heart to see Rustin so dejected.

"Erm… Suppose I'll head out, then." Rustin turned on his heel and walked toward the door. "Unless—"

"Out." Karolina pointed to the door. "And don't you dare breathe a word of this to anyone until I've got that apothecary in irons, understand?"

"Of course, I…" He moved like he wanted to salute then perhaps realized he no longer had to. With a heavy sigh that shook his large frame, he slunk toward the door and was gone.

"I swear," Karolina muttered, pocketing his badge. "Should've pushed harder to do that a year ago. Maybe we could've put a pin in all the nonsense that's been going on. I've half a mind to call Dag Flanigan back here to test every person in town for magic."

"I believe Zed Mackey already did that," Bev said, leaving out that he'd given that job to Rustin, and he'd failed spectacularly at it. "So what do we do for law enforcement? Don't you need to confer with Mayor Hendry about this?"

"I don't need to confer with anyone," she snapped. "I outrank Hendry and everyone else in this town."

"Yes, but—"

"I'm not going to entertain more of your questions," she said. "The only thing I want to hear from you is where I can find the apothecary."

Bev stared at her, bewildered. "Well, if he's not here, I'd probably check his apartment upstairs. But otherwise, I haven't a clue where he might've gone off to."

Karolina narrowed her gaze. "Were *you* aware that Bernard was dealing with illegal magic? Gotten a few tinctures from him that might've had something extra?"

"Feel free to test me for magic," Bev said, crossing her arms over her chest.

"Then why are you protecting him?"

"I'm not protecting anyone," Bev said. "But I doubt arresting an innocent person is going to stop the attacks."

"He's not innocent." Karolina waved the bag around. "He's got an illegal substance. What's to say he's not using it to attack people then cure them?"

"To what end?"

"I don't care about the end."

Bev narrowed her eyes. "I would've thought you'd learned your lesson with those sinkholes. You can't go around ruining people's lives in your zealous desire to carry out Her Majesty's orders."

"I can, and I will continue to do so," she said. "There is *nothing* more important than clearing out these magical creatures. They're a danger to society, a danger to Her Majesty, and a danger to anyone who swore to protect her. Now, if you don't tell me where the apothecary is, I'm going to have to take *you* away in irons."

Bev stared at her, knowing full well Karolina would make good on her threats. Bernard *did* have illegal magic, even if he was using it to help people.

"Bernard isn't responsible," Stella said from the front door to the front room. "Because he *just* left here, saying he had a cure."

"So I can find him at the inn?" Karolina asked.

Stella squeaked, realizing too late her mistake. "But he's not—"

"You'd better keep to your mixing," Karolina said. "I'll be back to test *you* for magic when I'm done with Bernard."

~

Bev hoped Stella had some iron-infused tea sitting around, but following Karolina was more important. The soldier was more interested in any result, even if that result wasn't the right one. She'd shown she'd do whatever it took to find what she was looking for, having caused sinkholes and earthquakes all over town. Could she have been behind the curses to…what? Fire Rustin? That seemed awfully cruel, and while Karolina had proven herself that, Rustin shouldn't have even been a consideration to her.

The soldier burst into the inn then stopped. Bev, a few steps behind her, soon realized why.

Etheldra, Max, Eldred, Trent, and Herman sat in the front room of the inn, sipping on tea and looking no worse for the wear. Herman and Trent sat on opposite sides of the room, glaring at each other, but everyone else looked like they were coming to their senses.

"What—"

Earl burst from the backroom, kettle in hand and the brightest smile on his face. "Who needs more tea?"

"Me," Etheldra said, weakly raising her cup.

Earl bustled over to serve her then walked around adding more to the cups of those who requested it. A moment later, he noticed Karolina and Bev standing in the doorway, shell-shocked.

"What happened?" Bev asked. "Did they wake up?"

"Bernard found the cure," Earl said with a bright smile. "It worked immediately. I couldn't believe it when Etheldra sat up."

"*I* can't believe someone cursed me," she snapped. She went back to sipping her tea until she noticed Karolina standing next to Bev. "Eh? What are you doing back in town, soldier? Here to cause more sinkholes?"

Bev's heart warmed at Etheldra's bluntness, even if it did earn a scowl from Karolina. "So, miraculously, you all woke up, eh?" Karolina asked.

"It is a miracle." Doc Howser walked in behind Earl, holding a basket of carrots. "I hope you don't mind, Bev. These poor folks are starving. They ate all the muffins already."

"No, please," Bev said, walking over. "Whatever we can do. I can ask the butchers for something quick to feed them. Sausage, perhaps? I—"

"Enough of this," Karolina snapped. "Where's that apothecary?"

Howser lifted his head. "Why?"

"I found illegal magical ingredients in his shop," Karolina said. "And he's under arrest."

"Clearly, those magical ingredients were the trick to saving them," Earl said, tightening his grip on the tea kettle. "I think that's worth overlooking their supposed illegality, don't you?"

"Her Majesty doesn't see it that way," Karolina said. "Now, where is he—"

"Where's who?" Bernard said, appearing behind Howser. He once again looked like he hadn't slept in days, his hair sticking out at all angles.

Karolina smiled like a predator. "Bernard Rickshaw, you are under arrest for the illegal possession of magical items."

"W-what?" Bernard took a step back. "I don't —"

"Now see here!" Etheldra rose sharply then swayed and sat back down, gripping her head. "You can't arrest him. He's the reason we're all awake."

"And probably the cause of it, too," Karolina said.

"I would *never*," Bernard said, putting his hand over his chest. "I've spent all this time trying to—"

"Enough." She pulled out a pair of glowing cuffs. "Let's go."

Bev stepped forward. "Taking him away is only going to cause more problems. The person who cursed these folks is still out there. Bernard's the only one who can cure them. Do you want the whole town to go under—"

"What I *want* is—"

Bev swayed, feeling like she'd fallen asleep for a brief moment, then steadied herself. Her attention went back to Bernard—but he was gone.

"What in the...?" Karolina, who looked as befuddled as everyone else, asked, "Where did he go? What in the world happened?"

"Bernard!" Howser exclaimed, taking a step back. "What kind of sorcery is—?"

"Which one of you did this?" Karolina said, looking around the room like a wild woman.

"Well, I don't think any of us did," Bev said slowly. "I don't even know what..."

But she did. Although the last time she'd seen something like this, she'd been on the other side, where she'd had a long conversation before the caster had left to go back to Lower Pigsend. But Bev didn't want to say anything, not until she knew why.

"I think you should probably go catch him," Earl said, mildly.

"Run fast," Etheldra said with a smirk. "Seems like he got a good head start."

Karolina looked around, perhaps calculating who she might arrest in lieu of Bernard, but then, with a huff, she ran out the door.

~

All other concerns could wait, as Bev wanted to make sure the newly awoken victims were well-fed and had as much tea as they could stomach. Word, of course, spread fast about their miraculous recovery, as well as Bernard's mysterious disappearance. Ida, who brought over a large helping of sausage for Bev to fry up, flittered around, sharing the joy that everyone was back to normal—and even more joy that the Harvest Festival wasn't going to be canceled.

"I'm not so sure about that," Bev said, bringing out the first round of sausage to each of the victims. "We still don't know who cursed them—or why. Karolina only wanted to arrest Bernard because he had illegal substances."

"Yes, but he ran," Ida said. "Why would he run if he wasn't guilty?"

"Why would he cure them if he was?" Earl shot back.

"Bah, it's too loud in here," Eldred announced, standing slowly. "I'm going home."

"You can't," Howser said, standing from where he'd been checking Trent's pulse. "You're weak. You've got to stay here and eat something. I'm sure we can fetch a wagon to get you home—"

He waved his hand. "I'm fine. Fit as a fiddle. Been sleeping too long as it is. Need to get back home and check on my crops." He put his hands on his hips. "Those molepeople probably got to my wheat already. Confound it. They're sneaky like that. I'm sure they're responsible for all this trouble."

Bev glanced around. No one else seemed to take him seriously, which was a good thing. But Bev still didn't want him to leave before asking him a few questions.

"Erm, about that," Bev said. "Did you see who cursed you? Or hear anything before it happened? I'm worried someone might try again, especially now that Bernard and his cure are gone."

"Not a thing." He shook his head. "I was sitting in my chair. I'd spent the morning weeding my garden, so my back was aching. Took a little tincture. Next thing I know, I'm standing here."

Exactly as Bev had thought. "Thank you, I—"

"You took a tincture?" Herman asked, furrowing his brow. "From Bernard?"

Eldred nodded. "Nothing I haven't gotten a thousand times from him before."

"Well, I got, erm, something new from him," Herman said, glancing around as he spoke. "Something to keep *pests* out of my garden." He glared at Trent. "I'd put it down an hour before, then came to check on my pumpkins. Saw a droplet on one of the pumpkins and touched it. Next thing, I'm waking up here at the inn, no clue what happened."

Bev turned, shocked. "What?"

"Yeah, what?" Trent snarled. "You cheatin', Herman?"

"Oh, you're one to talk," Bev said. "Bernard told me you asked for a potion to help your pumpkins grow." She thumbed at Herman. "Herman's, at least, was to keep out pests." She declined to elaborate that both tinctures were magical.

"Yeah, like *you*," Herman snapped to Trent. "And what's the big idea, getting a tincture to cheat? You think you have any shot—"

"I also had touched one of his vials," Max said slowly. "It was sitting on top of the book I was retrieving for you, Bev."

All eyes swept to Etheldra, who'd been silent.

She glared back at them. "I may or may not have taken something ten minutes before I collapsed. But I ain't gonna tell you about it."

"What were you—" Ida asked with a chuckle.

"*None of your business, girl.*"

"So," Bev said, bringing the conversation back to the topic at hand, "every one of you had touched the potion Bernard gave you right before you fainted? But Eldred was the only one who took it immediately before, right?"

They all nodded.

"What are you thinking, Bev?" Earl asked. "Could Bernard have been behind it after all? He did run."

"No," Howser said. "No, we're looking for a curse. That's what you said, right, Bev?"

She let out a small gasp as all the pieces came together in her mind. She blinked for a moment, holding onto the nebulous thought as it made sense, but also *didn't*, and opened and closed her mouth a few times.

"I'll be right back."

With Biscuit at her heels, Bev sprinted through town. It was too much of a coincidence. Bernard certainly hadn't been the one to curse them, but it was clear someone wanted to make it seem that way. Of course, that discovery would've only come after all the victims awoke. So someone wanted Bernard to get the ingredients he needed to cure them only for the victims to turn on him.

Bev had asked herself who the culprit was trying to send a message to, and she didn't think it was a coincidence Karolina Hunter had shown up in town, eager to arrest anyone. Whoever had framed Bernard wanted him arrested, but…

…but had also orchestrated his saving.

Percival was the only one Bev had seen cast that kind of magic before, when he'd come to grab Nog for causing problems in the dark forest. And to her knowledge, he was the only one who *could* slow down an entire room to rescue an apothecary.

Not only that, but Shamus had groused about the horrible job Gerry was doing. Had Percival masterminded the entire thing to convince Bernard to take shelter in Lower Pigsend? That seemed awfully cruel for the kindly wizard, even if it did mean Bernard would be safe from Her Majesty. But that also meant Pigsend would be without a main apothecary.

Still, she held off her anger until she knew more. There *had* to be a good explanation. There had to be solid reasoning that would make all this make sense. Perhaps Percival hadn't known about what was going on. Perhaps Shamus had lied, perhaps…

She rounded the corner, headed toward the tunnel where she knew she'd find Shamus, though she couldn't even be sure it was open. As she ran by

Eldred's house, out onto the fields, and crested the hill, the tunnel was indeed open, but Shamus was nowhere to be found.

"Let's go, Biscuit," Bev huffed.

She marched through the tunnel, walking down, down, down in the darkness. Her hands shook with fury until she heard voices up ahead.

"Shamus?" Bev called. "Shamus, if that's you, you have a *lot* of explaining to do!"

She turned a corner in the tunnel, expecting to reach Lower Pigsend, but instead found herself in a small cavern filled with people. It took her a moment to recognize the faces in the dark, but one by one she did. Freddie and Hans Silver. Vellora. Gore. And one other person, with broad shoulders, a dark, bald head, and a commanding presence, standing with his back to her.

"It was you," Bev gasped, taking a step back.

Andres Rade, Vellora's commander, turned around with a smile. "Bev! What took you so long?"

Chapter Twenty~One

"What...in the world is going on?" Bev managed.

Andres...was in Lower Pigsend. Well, not exactly, but close enough. He clearly knew about Shamus's tunnel, so it stood to reason he knew about the rest of it, too.

"Where's Shamus?" Bev asked. "And Percival?"

"I'd wager Percival is helping the good folks of Lower Pigsend, as he does. Shamus is presumably getting Bernard settled in his new home," Andres said, as if all that were perfectly logical. "Come in, Bev. I'm sure you have a lot of questions. I'm happy to answer as many as I can."

Bev took the final few steps to join the group in

the cave, standing next to Vellora, who shrunk next to her. "How long have you—"

"I don't know what's going on," she said, holding up her hands. "All I know is I got a message from Andres to meet today, then he led us to this tunnel. He was about to tell us what's going on when you showed up."

"I was hoping you'd figure it out, especially when Bernard disappeared," Andres said, smiling at her like a proud uncle. "You are a very clever innkeeper."

Bev ignored the compliment, glaring at Gore, who was directly across from her. "*You* lied to me."

"I also have no idea what was going on," he said, holding up his hands. "Like Vellora, I was in my shop, got the message, and I'm as in the dark as you."

Bev pointed to her ears. "Didn't overhear a conversation or two?"

"I told you, I've been in the forge," Gore said, showing her his calloused hands. "See? I've done many bad things in my life, but I didn't lie to you." He nodded to Freddie and Hans. "I figure I lied to them, so they could lie to me."

Bev turned to the two farmers, realization dawning. "You… Hans. You're the mage. You're the one who's been cursing everyone. You took the potion to enhance your powers and cursed them."

"Guilty," Hans said with a nervous smile. "I

only agreed to it because Andres promised me they'd be fine. It was a harmless sleeping curse."

"Harmless, yeah, except they weren't breathing or—" Bev started. "You *hurt* people, Andres! It's like those confounded blackmail letters—"

"And had *that* plan worked, we wouldn't have had to go *this* route," Andres said, glancing at Freddie.

"Then *you* should've told me that was the plan," Freddie snapped, "instead of dangling my husband in front of Dag Flanigan."

"*That* wasn't part of the plan, either," Andres said, giving Gore a dirty look. "Regardless, all's well that ends well, and everyone is fine."

"I'm sorry. I just can't get past the fact that you two willingly cursed people. Your own neighbors!" Bev said. "What in the world were you thinking?"

"It's quite simple. We needed Rustin fired," Andres said.

"W-what?" Bev blinked. *That* certainly wasn't on her list of possible motives. "Why? What has he ever done to—?"

"The reason for it will come," Andres said simply. "But our plans require the sheriff's position to be empty."

Bev shook her head. Of all the reasons… "Andres, this is beyond the pale. People were scared out of their minds. I've spent the last few days running all over town looking for a culprit. The least you could've done was tell me what you were planning—"

"Or you could've sat this one out," Andres said. "*You* don't have to be the one investigating everything. Had you stayed out of the way and let Rustin flail about, we might not have had to curse so many people."

Bev's eyes narrowed. "So you're saying it's my fault?"

"Actually, no." Andres once again leveled a glare, this time at Freddie and Hans. "My instructions were to make it obvious from the outset that the apothecary was to blame. Which is hard to do if the tincture vials aren't found anywhere near the victims, *Freddie.* "

"Well?" Freddie's face turned red. "They got him eventually."

"*Correction*," Andres said, with more than a little frustration, "Karolina Hunter merely found magical ingredients in his shop and arrested him."

"All's well that ends well," Hans said. "Isn't that what you said?"

She blinked, realizing she hadn't even considered Freddie and Hans as suspects, though she should have. They lived near Eldred and Trent. "Why Eldred? Did it have anything to do with Officer Nog?"

"Erm, no," Hans said. "I saw your dog headed to his house, so I thought it was a good opportunity to set a better crime scene this time."

Bev closed her eyes. Poor Eldred. "I can't believe you two would attack your own neighbors. This is… This is abhorrent."

Freddie stammered, but Hans puffed out his chest. "They were *fine*. Safe and well. And it gave me a chance to flex my magic a bit, so yeah. I leapt at the chance. Gonna need all the practice I can get."

"Why?" Bev said. "Practice for what? And *why* was Bernard framed?"

"The target's always been Rustin," Andres said. "But we settled on using Bernard as the lure to get Karolina in town, because there would be a nice, safe place for him to land where his skills would be highly coveted."

"Lower Pigsend," Bev said. "You've been talking with Shamus, haven't you? How did you even know it existed?"

"Gore alerted me to the *wonderful* town of Lower Pigsend a few weeks ago, though it took me some time to find this tunnel," Andres said. "I'd hoped to recruit more magical creatures to our cause, but predictably, the denizens of Lower Pigsend wanted nothing to do with a burgeoning rebellion. At least, Shamus didn't want to share the news until there was something *to* share."

Bev stopped herself from applauding Shamus, as it was clear he'd had a hand in this. "Did he make the potion Hans took to curse people?"

"He gave us the recipe," Andres said. "And a gentleman who could procure the ingredients, though I'd already heard of Winston in my circles. It was complex, but nothing I couldn't handle." He smiled. "If you'll recall, I'm the one who taught Zed Mackey everything he knows."

Bev exhaled through her nose. "So Shamus gave you a recipe, and he gets an apothecary who knows what he's doing?"

"They got the better end of the deal, if you ask me. Their current apothecary's skills left a lot to be desired, and the chance to have someone with the breadth and knowledge Bernard has...well, he was grateful for the trade."

Bev clicked her tongue. "I don't suppose you've let Bernard know of this *plan*."

"No, but he was overjoyed to get a savior in Shamus when Karolina Hunter tried to arrest him," Andres said with a smile. "And gladly took up his invitation to Lower Pigsend."

So it was Shamus who cast the time-pausing spell. "And Gerry?" Bev asked. "What does he get out of this?"

"Who?" Andres said.

"Bernard's brother. The other apothecary in Lower Pigsend," Bev said. "Did you give him a chance to escape?"

"Shamus didn't mention that the other apothecary was related to Bernard," Andres said.

"Suppose they're down there together now."

"Can't wait to hear how *that* reunion went," Bev muttered.

"Oh, Bernard's in a safe place where he can openly practice his magical abilities without fear of being arrested," Andres said, as if he hadn't cost Bernard his shop, his home, and his friends in Pigsend. "Besides that, if things keep as they are, he won't be in Lower Pigsend for long."

"What's that supposed to mean?" Bev asked.

Andres smiled. "I do hate to keep pushing off your questions, but that one I can't answer directly. I do promise that all will be revealed in the coming weeks."

Her anger boiling over, Bev took a step forward, poking her finger into Andres's chest with all the fury she could muster. "Listen *here*. I don't care if you're planning to do something to the queen herself. You will *cease* your machinations in Pigsend, else I will tell the first queen's soldier I see all about your plans. Blackmail letters are one thing, but hurting the innocent people in my town? I won't stand for it." She glared at Vellora, Gore, Freddie, and Hans. "And you four should stand with me instead of with him."

"I understand you're angry with me," Andres said, gently removing Bev's finger. "But you have to understand that what I'm doing is for the greater good. A small amount of pain now for a revolutionary change later." He gestured toward the door. "Karolina Hunter spared no quarter when she found Bernard's magical things, right?"

"And you made sure she found them," Bev said.

He smiled. "Bev, you're missing the point. Soldiers like Karolina… They don't care who they hurt. She was happy to find *any* kind of magical evidence, and any kind of culprit to haul away. She didn't care if it stopped the attacks, only that she *did* something to show her queen she was being proactive. You should be thanking me that it was Bernard and not your pobyd friends next door."

Bev opened and closed her mouth. He had a point, but she didn't want to give him the satisfaction.

"I care about the people I'm hurting," Andres said. "I made Shamus swear up and down that this curse would keep the victims safe. And I was the one who gave Winston the ingredient Bernard needed to cure them." He smiled. "And the five victims are awake, are they not?"

"Yes, but—"

"And healthy?"

"Yes, but…" Bev stomped her foot. "We could have really thought they were dead! It's a good thing Howser knew—" She stopped. "Did you send Howser, too?"

"I knew he was around," he said. "And that he'd accurately diagnose the magical comas for what they were. Which he did. Brilliantly."

"That doesn't excuse the fear you caused in town," Bev said, thinking of the worried faces at the town meeting.

"A little fear I can live with," he said.

Bev felt like throttling him. "Whatever you're doing, it's not important enough to cause this much chaos—"

"But it is, Bev, that's what you don't understand." He let out a breath. "And unfortunately, this is where the explanations will have to end. We have lots to discuss, and a lot of plans to define. So…" He gestured toward the door. "If you'll excuse us."

Bev exhaled loudly. "I'm not going anywhere, Andres. Freddie and Hans need to be punished for what they've done." She screwed up her face. "I'm going to Karolina—"

"If you do," he said slowly, "I'm afraid I have no choice but to tell *her* about your past."

Bev's heart stopped as she stared at him. Had she not been furious about the curses, she might've stopped long enough to ask him the questions that had been burning in her chest the past few months. "You said you don't know anything."

"I said I didn't have anything to share," he said, and she scowled at the word choice. "And I still don't. Because it's not time for your part in this larger production." He smiled. "However, if you jeopardize our plans, I won't hesitate to inform all the pertinent people of your past. Rest assured, they will be *most* happy to find you." He nodded to Vellora. "I've got someone across the street to keep an eye on you."

Bev looked at Vellora, but the butcher wouldn't quite meet her gaze. "Vellora? Do you know anything about my—"

"No one does but me," he said. "Which is how I want it to remain." His smile was genuine, and there was almost a little pity in his eyes. "I know it's frustrating, all the times I've pushed you off. But the time for the truth is coming, and when it arrives, I'll tell you more than you want to know. But for now… This is goodbye."

~

Bev fumed over the revelations all the way back to town. She couldn't understand how Freddie and Hans could live with themselves. Sure, everyone was safe, sure, everyone was healthy, but something had to be done about their subterfuge. She stood outside the inn for a moment, knowing she couldn't come barreling in furious without arousing suspicion. She stared in the window, watching Earl and Etheldra talking with dewy eyes and Trent and Herman at least civilly discussing something with Max.

"What did you find out?"

Bev jumped as Hendry came up beside her. "Nothing."

"Doesn't look like nothing. Looks like you found the culprit and can't do anything about it."

Bev exhaled. "Rustin's been fired."

"So he told me. He's blubbering in my office right now. I had to leave him there to get a break."

"Are you going to reinstate him?" Bev asked.

"Ms. Hunter informs me that's not within my purview at the moment," she said. "Apparently, *she's* going to stick around and keep the peace during the Harvest Festival."

Bev turned to her. "What?" That couldn't have been in Andres's plan. Or was it? He did seem to anticipate *everything*.

"One hopes she'll move on after the festival concludes, but it'll be a long month until then." Hendry sighed. "Suppose we'd all better keep eating that iron crisp to stay safe."

"Suppose so," Bev said.

"So who are we going to blame this on?" Hendry asked. "Bernard? Seems a likely candidate, especially after everyone said they'd had a potion."

"He didn't do it," Bev said.

"Yes. That's obvious. But he's a very good scapegoat." Hendry surveyed Bev. "Are the attacks going to stop?"

"I believe so, yes." If their goal was to get Rustin fired, that had been accomplished. Bev didn't see a reason for them to continue terrorizing the town, and Andres had made it seem like that part of their plan had concluded.

"Then we can get back to normal," Hendry replied with a satisfied smile. "All's well that—"

"But it's not *all well*," Bev said. "Earl probably lost three years of his life from worry. Bardoff hasn't been sleeping. The rest of the town has been beside themselves. I wasted several days running all over the place. We don't have an apothecary anymore—"

"That's not true. Stella's going to be busier than ever."

"How can you be so glib about this?" Bev asked.

"Well, unless you have something you want to share, or something you want me to act upon, we have to go forward with the truth as it is right now," Hendry said.

"And that is?"

"Well, it appears Bernard had a magical accomplice. That accomplice did the cursing, Bernard did the potion-making," Hendry said. "Perhaps so he could cure them and save the day."

Bev blinked at her. "That's not going to satisfy people."

"It will when the attacks stop," Hendry said. "That's all people really care about. It's like when those buildings collapsed last spring. We never did find out why, did we? But soon everyone moved on until the next thing happened." She smiled. "Not everything requires a neat resolution."

Bev certainly felt it did, but although she could

tell Hendry that Hans and Freddie were the culprits, based on a plan concocted by Andres to get Rustin fired, she kept those thoughts to herself. After all, she believed Andres when he said he'd tell the queen's people about Bev's past. And something told her that if he was threatening, then Bev's past might be worth more than Andres's head.

"Well, that's settled then," Hendry said. "Suppose I'd better go mop Rustin up. He may not be sheriff anymore, but he's got to handle security for the festival."

"I thought Karolina was doing that?" Bev said.

"I'm sure she'll have her hands full doing other things," Hendry said.

Bev furrowed her brow. "Like what?"

"All in due time, Bev. Now, where are those bakers? I want to see about getting Rustin a pick-me-up. Can't have him crying in my office for the next month…"

Bev watched her go, still feeling unfulfilled. "One question."

"Hm?" Hendry spun around.

Bev considered her words carefully. "Why would someone want Rustin fired?"

Hendry's eyes widened, as if the question caught her completely off guard. She thought about it for a moment, putting her hands on her hips as she stared at the ground.

"I have no idea."

Chapter Twenty~Two

"I hereby call this meeting of the Harvest Festival Planning Committee to order," Ida said. "And a good thing, too. We're a week behind schedule."

Once again, Bev, Ida, Hendry, and Lillie met in the dining room of the Weary Dragon to discuss the upcoming Harvest Festival. Rustin, who Hendry *insisted* would still be in charge of security, was wallowing at home.

"Are you sure he's going to be able to handle security?" Ida asked.

"I doubt he's going to be the only one handling security," Hendry said. "But it's something to keep his chin up, so let's just let him have it."

It had been a few days since everyone had woken up, and Bev still hadn't quite gotten over not being able to give everyone a satisfactory answer. But, as Hendry had predicted, the people of Pigsend accepted that Bernard was the bad guy, and everyone proclaimed they were well rid of him. It bothered Bev more than she cared to admit, but she couldn't say anything—not even to Lillie.

"Bev?" Ida's voice snapped Bev back to the room.

"Yes? Sorry." Bev smiled. "What were you saying?"

"We need to gather tables for the judging," Ida said. "Can you talk with Bardoff to see if he can spare some? I know he lost a few when his schoolhouse collapsed earlier this year. Maybe Etheldra could spare a few from the tea shop, too."

"I doubt it," Hendry said. "The Harvest Festival is one of her busiest weeks. She'll need every table she has."

"Then maybe, Bev, you could spare—"

"Can't," Bev said. "Same story here."

"Fine." Ida huffed. "If all else fails, we can use our dining room table. I'm sure Vellora won't mind."

At the mention of Vellora, Bev's mood darkened once more. She hadn't been able to look the other butcher in the eye, nor had Vellora been around much. Was she preparing for Andres's big plan, or was she hiding because she was guilty?

"Bev, goodness me," Ida said, waving her hand in front of Bev's face. "Are you well? You haven't been the same since everyone woke up."

"I'm fine," Bev said. "What is it you were saying?"

"I was asking if you'd be kind enough to pop over to the schoolhouse and check on the tables for us," Ida said.

Bev, grateful for the chance to stretch her legs instead of listening to the Harvest Festival plans, was happy to oblige. Biscuit followed at her heels; he hadn't left her side since everything had happened.

She passed her reflection in the bakery window. There was a permanent scowl on her face, it seemed. But she couldn't shake her mood. Everything felt grossly unfair, and she resented not being told the entire truth by everyone—especially Andres.

She walked to the town square and was pleasantly surprised to see Ramone Comely, but more surprised to see a gargantuan dragon fountain. Bev stared at it a minute, trying to recall how the old one had looked.

"It's magnificent, isn't it?" Ramone said, coming to stand next to Bev. "Just awe-inspiring. I finished it in the spring but never got the okay to put it up. Hendry popped by yesterday and told me my window to do so was closing. So I hopped to it."

"Does it work?" Bev asked.

Ramone nodded and pointed to the pump that hadn't been used in some time. "You pump it here. Once it gets going, it'll keep recycling water in perpetuity—or until another sinkhole eats it." They beamed at Bev. "What do you think?"

"It's beautiful." The sculptor was kind, and Bev didn't see a need to share her bad mood with them. "Is your brother still around?"

"The fiend decided to take his talents back to Kaiser Tuckey's," Ramone said with a sigh. "But rest assured, we're quite close still. We plan on visiting each other once a month to keep our creativity fresh."

"I'm glad to hear it."

"Something's wrong." Ramone frowned at her. "You're not your usual self, Bev. Is it all the attacks? Have they set you wrong?"

"You could say that," Bev said.

"Well, we can all be happy that perfidious Bernard has been run out of town," they said. "Glad I never took a tincture from him. Could you imagine how the town would take it? To have me, Ramone Comely, master sculptor, asleep like that?"

"Unthinkable," Bev said lightly. "But it seems we're all safe now."

"Yes, indeed." They sighed again. "Onward to the Harvest Festival!"

They had lots to do, so Bev left them and continued to the schoolhouse. Bardoff was teaching in front of a chalkboard, and Bev was pleased to see his room full of children again.

"Now, children, continue tracing your letters," he said as soon as he spotted Bev. "Give me one minute." He crossed the small schoolhouse and shook Bev's hand. "Is everything all right?"

"Fine, fine. Ida wanted me to ask if you could spare a few tables for the Harvest Festival judging at the town hall," Bev said.

"Oh, erm." He looked around. There didn't seem to *be* a spare table in the room, as every one had a child seated in front of it. "Maybe. For how long?"

"The duration of the festival," Bev said.

He shook his head. "I'm sorry. I don't think I can. Maybe ask Etheldra?"

~

Although Bev knew it would be a dead end, she still went over there next. Shasta was working the front room, which looked a little more decorated than the last time Bev had been here. But more surprising were Trent and Herman sitting at the table with Doc Howser and…

"Sherry?" Bev sputtered. "Erm, I mean, Penny."

"It's fine, Bev," she said. "We've all gotten everything out in the open. Right, boys?"

Trent and Herman grumbled, both red-faced. On the table was the locket Bev had found on Herman's person. Howser sat next to his wife, holding her hand as she calmly looked at the two farmers.

"So…what's happening?" Bev asked slowly.

"My husband made me aware that both of these gents had left me their farms," she said. "I have *no* desire to inherit them, nor do I want to deal with them. So we've all come to agree that Trent and Herman will update their wills and select someone else to inherit their property."

Bev turned to Herman and Trent. "And you two…agree to this?"

"I don't see why I gotta," Trent said. "I was the last one who—"

"Trent, that was *forty* years ago," she said. "Goodness me, move on already."

His face burned.

Herman snorted at him, earning a scowl from Sherry. "Don't you start. My husband's going to check to make sure you speak with Max before the week is out."

"And what if I don't?" Herman snapped.

"Then I'll sell your property to Trent," Sherry said. "Or vice versa."

They both gasped in horror, breaking into almost identical speeches about how the other wouldn't know the first thing about growing their crops—or pumpkins, for that matter. That dissolved into them arguing over the best way to grow pumpkins, which resulted in Sherry and Howser rising from the table.

"Well, I'm…glad that's resolved," Bev said. "I'll be sure to tell Max to expect them."

"You're a gem, Bev," Howser said with a wink. "How are things at the inn?"

"Fine, fine," Bev said. "Quiet."

Howser had left the same day everyone woke, presumably going back to his bride in Middleburg. She debated asking him if he thought Bernard was guilty, but that might open questions that she didn't want to answer. Based on his awkward silence, he was perhaps thinking the same thing.

"I'm sorry for the abrupt greeting the other day," Sherry said, breaking the silence. "No one's ever recognized me before. I suppose it was inevitable, but I was hopeful maybe…" She shook her head. "In any case, thank you for bringing to light the inheritance issue. That would've been a nasty surprise."

"You really don't want anything to do with them, do you?" Bev said.

She glanced at the table, where the two farmers were still squabbling. "Not a thing."

"Will you two *knock it off!*" Etheldra barreled out of the back room. "You haven't been in town one day, Sher, and you've already brought this filth into my shop."

Sherry's face tightened. "I'm glad you're all right, Eth. But you're right, I should be getting on my way."

"Did you know I'd married?" Etheldra asked.

"I'm sorry?" Sherry frowned. "I—yes. I'd heard it through the grapevine. Congratulations. Earl is a lovely man."

"Better than I deserve, I tell you," Etheldra said, looking almost chastened. "Look, I know we never saw eye to eye on anything…"

"That's an understatement."

"But I hated that you disappeared," Etheldra said. "I thought about you every day, you know?"

"I thought about you, too," she said with a sad face. "I'm glad you have the shop, and Earl. And I hear you're retiring soon." She inhaled. "Maybe you can pay me a visit in Middleburg?"

"Middleburg? I hate that cesspool of a…" Etheldra stopped herself when Bev cleared her throat loudly. "What I mean to say is that I'd love to."

Sherry smiled then left with Howser. Etheldra stormed over to Trent and Herman and all but threw them out of the shop. The farmers skulked away to their opposite sides of town, and Etheldra let out a loud huff.

"Maybe it was a blessing I was asleep. Least I didn't have to listen to their squabbling," she grumbled. "Whatdya need, Bev?"

"Oh!" Bev had all but forgotten. "Ida's asking about spare tables for the Harvest Festival. Do you have any?"

"Ask the boss." Etheldra thumbed at Shasta.

"We don't," the twin replied. "But I think my sister has a few spare ones at the apothecary."

~

Stella was hard at work at the front counter, mixing ingredients to fill a set of five vials beside her. She looked up when Bev walked in, then went right back to her work. There was a line of tension on her face, and the circles under her eyes told Bev she hadn't slept much in the past few days.

"Shasta told me you'd be willing to part with a table," Bev said, cutting right to it. "For the Harvest Festival."

"In the back." She straightened. "You'll have to clean it off first."

Bev wasn't sure what she meant until she walked into the back room where Bernard had tested all the possible potions to cure everyone. It looked as though Karolina had searched this place thoroughly and hadn't taken much care to ensure that any of Bernard's vials were preserved.

"She comes by once a day," Stella said glumly. "Wants to test every potion I make. She was sure I was dealing with magic, too. Tested me with a prick to the finger."

"And?" Bev asked.

"Well, I'm still here, aren't I?" Stella said. After a moment, she glanced around furtively. "May have been enjoying a nice iron-infused crisp since Bernard was arrested. Or almost arrested."

"Good thinking," Bev said. "I'm so sorry. Are you doing all right?"

"I'm making do. It's funny. We used to be so busy. But my workload seems the same." She snorted. "Maybe Bernard was busy doing all the magical stuff Karolina accused him of and left me with all the mundane potions. Either way, I haven't seen the huge influx in orders I was expecting."

Perhaps because Bernard was still making them, and Winston was delivering them via Shamus. But it was better Stella didn't know that.

"I had a hunch he was doing something like that, but in this town, who *isn't* dabbling in magic, you know? I didn't think he was hurting anyone." She screwed up her face, as if she were trying not to cry. "I still don't. He didn't curse those people. Because it was a curse, wasn't it?"

Bev didn't know how to respond except to tell her to keep her chin up.

The back room of the apothecary had two tables that could be spared. Bev decided *Ida* would be the one to retrieve them, as Bev couldn't even fathom carrying them across town. With that sorted, she took her time returning to the inn, still feeling quite unmoored by the whole thing.

Andres had been so sure no one had been hurt,

but Stella certainly looked hurt. Bernard's reputation had been tarnished. And Rustin, for better or worse, had lost his job.

The sheriff was walking aimlessly around town, wearing a tunic that looked like it had been in a rainstorm. His eyes were red, and he carried a handkerchief as he padded down the street.

"Are you all right?" Bev asked.

"Fine, fine." He blew into the kerchief. "Glad Karolina left town for the moment."

"She's coming back," Bev said gently. "She said she's taking over for you."

"Yeah." He sniffed. "Good. Can't imagine I want to be involved with that anyway."

Bev patted him on the shoulder. "But you're still helping us with the festival, aren't you? That'll cheer you up."

He nodded. "I'm so thankful to you and Mayor Hendry. My only friends in town. You know, I can't help but feel this was a personal attack."

Bev licked her lips. "Why do you say that?"

"Well, how random it was. And how it all stopped when I got fired." He shook his head. "Hendry says I'm making too much out of it. But if they were tryin' to send a message, maybe the message was for me to quit sheriffin'."

"I wouldn't think about it too much," Bev managed. "It's a new opportunity. An open window, if you will. A chance to find something else to fill your days. Maybe you could become a farmer, you know?

"I hate dirt." He snorted. "But maybe you're right."

"Start by coming to the committee meeting," Bev said. Maybe if Rustin was there, Bev could skip out on the rest of the planning. "I'm sure we can use you more than we are."

Rustin seemed bolstered by the idea, and threaded his arm through Bev's as they walked back to the Weary Dragon. She was rather hoping the meeting would've disbanded, but everyone was still around the center table.

"Rustin, so nice of you to join us," Ida said, pushing out a chair for him. "Have a seat. Bev, what of the tables?"

"Two at the apothecary shop," Bev said.

"Don't mention the apothecary!" Rustin wailed, crying into his hands.

Hendry glared at Bev as if it were her fault and patted Rustin on the back. "Now I have to listen to him blubber here."

"Here." Lillie slid over one of the muffins she'd brought. "Have a muffin."

Rustin took a bite and instantly relaxed, a smile curling onto his face. "That's great. Thank you. I don't know what you put in it—"

"Yeah, what *did* you put in it?" Ida asked.

"Love," Lillie said with a bright smile.

"Anyway, we were discussing the schedule of events," Ida said. "Bev, it's good you've returned. As I was telling Hendry, I really liked the way we had it last year, so I don't think we should change, except for maybe a few small tweaks here and there. I know things were a little crazy because of all the chaos, but having the final food judging on the last day worked well, don't you think?"

"Unfortunately, the final schedule's going to have to remain a *bit* in flux," Hendry said, sounding very much like she'd rather be talking about something else.

"Why do you say that?" Ida asked. "Is there something I've missed?"

"Erm, yes." Hendry tapped her fingers on the table. "There is one more thing."

"What?" Bev asked, her heart sinking.

"It's that..." Hendry cleared her throat. "Well, happily, Pigsend's going to be playing host to a very special guest for this year's festival."

"Who?"

"Queen Meandra."

Bev concludes her adventures in

Acknowledgments

As always, first thanks goes to my husband, for supporting me, believing in me, and being my rock during the difficult season of two very small children and me trying to take on the world. Thanks must also go to my parents, my in-laws, and my aunt for being the world's best village and allowing me to keep writing with said very small children.

Thanks to Chelsea, Danielle, Lisa, and Lacey for being the all-star team who helps bring these beautiful books to life.

Finally, thanks go to the Sush Street Team for being the cheerleaders who love these books and continue to read everything I put out.

A MER-MURDER AT THE COVE

Jo Maelstrom's avoidance problems hit an all-time high when, after weeks of dodging her grandmother's calls, she got a text that "Big Jo" had died suddenly. Now back in Eldred's Hollow, a supernatural haven on the Gulf Coast of Alabama, Jo is forced to reckon with her past – and the severe lack of magic that sent her running in the first place. Her grandmother's bar and marina, Witch's Cove, is in some dire financial straits, and there's more than a few people itching to take it off her hands. But when the leader of the local mermaid clan washes up dead on the shore, Jo finds herself embroiled in the question of who and why – and does it have anything to do with her own grandmother's mysterious death?

A Mer-Murder at the Cove is the first book in the Witch's Cove Paranormal Cozy Mystery series

Also by the Author

The Seod Croi Chronicles

After her father's murder, princess Ayla is set to take the throne — but to succeed, she needs the magical stone her evil stepmother stole. Fortunately, wizard apprentice Cade and knight Ward are both eager to win Ayla's favor.

A Quest of Blood and Stone is the first book in the *Seod Croi* chronicles and is available now in eBook, paperback, and hardcover.

ALSO BY THE AUTHOR

THE MADION WAR TRILOGY

He's a prince, she's a pilot, they're at war. But when they are marooned on a deserted island hundreds of miles from either nation, they must set aside their differences and work together if they want to survive.

The Madion War Trilogy is a fantasy romance available now in eBook, Paperback, and Hardcover.

Also by the Author

Empath

Lauren Dailey is in break-up hell, but if you ask her she's doing just great. She hears a mysterious voice promising an easy escape from her problems and finds herself in a brand new world where she has the power to feel what others are feeling. Just one problem—there's a dragon in the mountains that happens to eat Empaths. And it might be the source of the mysterious voice tempting her deeper into her own darkness.

Empath is a stand-alone fantasy that is available now in eBook, Paperback, and Hardcover.

About the Author

S. Usher Evans was born and raised in Pensacola, Florida. After a decade of fighting bureaucratic battles as an IT consultant in Washington, DC, she suffered a massive quarter-life-crisis. She found fighting dragons was more fun than writing policy, so she moved back to Pensacola to write books full-time. She currently resides there with her husband and kids, and frequently can be found plotting on the beach.

Visit S. Usher Evans online at:
http://www.susherevans.com/